CW01648437

THE EARTH TRIP

Tock Von calmly watched them stretch the huge net beneath his tree. He saw the man in the uniform go and return with an odd gun cradled in his arms. He looked down at the command post the fuzz had established at a sufficiently safe distance from his tree and then up at the rising muzzle of the gun. He had a chilling moment of misgiving as he imagined crosshairs, himself frozen in their hairline juncture. But there were always risks involved in dealing with an alien species, he reminded himself. He was perfectly willing to take them. He rose up on his toes, gave Devlin a smart salute and waited for the drug dart to strike, planning on initiating peace talks later and presenting a persuasive argument for the reordering of certain earthly priorities.

Also by the same author,
and available in Coronet Books:

Mindmix

The Earth Tripper

Leo P. Kelley

CORONET BOOKS
Hodder Fawcett Ltd., London

First published 1973 by
Fawcett Publications Inc, New York
Coronet edition 1974

FOR BINKY

The characters and situations in this book are entirely imaginary and bear no relation to any real person or actual happening.

Printed and bound in Great Britain for
Coronet Books, Hodder Fawcett Ltd, ;
St. Paul's House, Warwick Lane,
London, EC4P 4AH,
By C. Nicholls & Company Ltd,
The Philips Park Press, Manchester M11 4AU

ISBN 0 340 18285 7

ONE

"Well, Tock Von, like I said,
I don't ball mutants."

Not normally a sidler, Tock Von nevertheless slyly sidled across the polished cocktail party floor where prowled the wild and the would-be wild. He slid past the miniskirts and the Daks, ducking "What do you do's?" and dodging indiscriminate and nonchalant gropings.

This was his sixth field trip to Earth. He had made up his mind that it would be different from his previous five. This one would not be limited to a specified amount of time as the others had been, nor would it be "spatially circumscribed within acceptable levels of contactive risk." At least, not for him. Not this time.

They had called him a rebel on his home planet, Eleison, almost from the minute he had enrolled in the program of Extra-Eleisonite Expeditions into Alien Galactic Territories by Means of Warp Continuum Exploitation. They said he was too daring, not conformist enough. Something of a malcontent, as a matter of fact.

They were right on all counts. Why, he had mentally asked himself, must he and the others taking the trips remain within circumscribed physical limits? How could they truly learn about the natives of Earth if they were not allowed to mix freely and without restrictions?

The older and more experienced members of the Extra-Eleisonite Expeditionary Force had answered that too much contact might prove problematical. Thus space/time limits were imposed on each member during the field trips. This time, this sixth time for Tock Von, they were researching the mores of a typical terrestrial cocktail party. No member of the EEF was allowed to leave the premises. They would remain on Earth for only four hours.

In uncharacteristic fashion when the plan had been outlined, Tock Von had kept his mouth shut. But he had made his plans.

Wandering on through the cocktail party room, he reeled past brittle girls breaking their laughter into careful quotas, an other-ended wind, because they didn't want to seem too eager for whatever. He slid past men with precision haircuts and polished eyes that told of barbs and bank accounts. He found himself thinking of the long evolutionary road a-winding up through salt seas—unicellular somethings swishing and sloshing about in Earth's primeval waves and then slipping out on beaches. "Air? Ugh!" An antiphonal unicellular response, "Don't knock it if you haven't tried it." And then, of course, in time, all in good time, the brontosaurus and the pterodactyl. Missing links and minor miracles. The opposable thumb and the wheel. A capsule history of Man.

The simulated human body he inhabited, Tock Von thought, glancing idly at himself—not really himself—in a gilded mirror, was an effective disguise and fairly efficient, although it couldn't compare with the evolutionary excellence of his normal Eleisonite body. Long hair, black—a concession to contemporary terrestrial times. Lean face. Muscles here and there. A soulful expression befitting the twenty-year-old male Caucasian he was supposed to be. He glanced at his wrist watch.

Ten minutes left.

The other members of the Force were sprinkled about the room. Talking. Talking.

Someone was talking of the wonderful way Cuba used

to be—sleek-eyed men in dim doorways whispering of erotica. But now—ah, well, revolution certainly had its virtues but, hell, increased sugar cane production was a rather shabby compensation for neon sex, don't you think? What do you do? Don't you think?

It was all very in, with it, together, now. In two words: New York. Under the elegant recessed lighting's fluorescing promise, Tock Von sidled on, making mental notes on Man.

Ah! Over there! He saw her sitting on the floor, on a purple pillow, with her legs crossed—*en garde!*—and fondling an ill-tempered Siamese cat. The cat pawed her finger cymbals, became momentarily entranced by her silver bracelets, then stalked away haughtily. She laughed. Did glasses shatter? Mirrors? Go over? Why not? Who knew what evil might lurk in the mind of a maiden?

He knelt down before her, a mendicant monk sandaled at a roadside shrine. He reached out, through the sheer cloud of sick-sweet smoke from the burning grass in her hand to touch with gentle brazenness her left nipple, which peeked eerily out at him from beneath the green silk of her see-through blouse.

He spun the prayer wheel of his head, hoping. "Would you like to know what I do?" he asked her. She had funky nostrils.

"I can tell."

"I mean besides that." She might, he thought, yep, she just might.

"My name is Gloria and I was a nun once. Well, a novice, to be exact."

"My name is Tock Von and I am from the Planet Eleison in the Sixteenth Star System of the Gamma Galaxy." Breaking his cover and not caring, breaking the first rule of the EEF. How did former nuns—novices, to be exact—do it? She might insist on incense and a lace surplice. Fetish fun!

"You must be a science-fiction freak," she remarked without enthusiasm.

"No, honest," he said, speaking sincerely through the smoke and her heavy scent. "It's true."

"Really? You look human to me. Except for those spooky gray eyes of yours."

Yeah, spooky gray eyes. Still—there had been a girl in Hoboken on his fourth field trip who had liked them a lot, kept the light on all the time just so she could see them during. Ancient history. "Sorry. Look at me only when I blink."

"If you're from another planet, how come you look human?"

"I'm passing."

"You're putting me on."

He shook his head and smiled sincerely. "It's the truth." Could she take it?

"Are you a head?" she asked suspiciously.

"No, an Eleisonite."

"I guess I see what you mean."

"You're very understanding, you know that?"

"Listen, man, you got an extra stick? I'm fresh out. I'll trade you. These bracelets and my finger cymbals for one lously little stick. Okay?"

"Well—"

"Just give it to me."

He quickly switched to the right nipple. "You really mean it?"

She got it. "No, I don't really mean it. I don't ball mutants."

"I'm not a mutant. I'm Tock Von from the Planet Eleison." He slipped on her bracelets, pocketed her finger cymbals, and passed her a stick.

"Well, Tock Von, like I said, I don't ball mutants."

He was hurt. He tried to explain, feeling his massive and by now familiar erection falter, that mutants had nothing to do with it. He was simply an alien.

"Okay, so you're an alien," she yipped, using the cold word as if she had just discovered it in a dictionary devoted to contemporary pornography. Well, aliens, she explained, puffing on the stick, were not her bag. She didn't go that route. It soon became apparent which route she went. She had been watching the dreamy girl across the room who was using an eyedropper to do esoteric things to her gin. He explained himself again, but she got up from her purple pillow and went over and spoke to the girl with the eyedropper whose name, he had learned earlier, was Angie Jean something. She was a waitress from New Rochelle who only came into the city on weekends "for a little speeding, a little sunshine."

The girls left together.

He made up his mind to forget Sister Sappho. Strange indeed, he thought, were the alien ways of humans. He looked at his watch. Two minutes and forty seconds left of this trip.

"Ready?" a sleekly coiffed woman whispered to him.

He nodded assent to the commander of the Extra-Eleisonite Expeditionary Force who was masquerading in her version of what an earthly movie star should look like. She wore a see-through blouse over her mammoth breasts and struggled earnestly with her top-heaviness.

A moment later, one by one, the Eleisonites slipped through the warp and were gone. Tock Von, with calm elan, waved goodby to them and headed for the door leading from the apartment.

The lusty commander of the EEF suddenly reappeared and seized his arm. They struggled.

"See you later," Tock Von told her, trying to break her wrestler's grip.

"The warp will decoalesce!" she warned him. "Delay can be fatal!"

"I'll take my chances," Tock Von declared, breaking free.

"Renegade!" the commander roared above the din of the party. "You're on report!"

Tock Von saluted her disappearance with a raised middle finger.

"Hey, where the hell did everybody go all of a sudden?" cried a drunken advertising executive.

"Here today, gone tomorrow," answered the blonde beside him who had one cool hand on his wallet.

Tock Von went out the door—on the run.

Passing.

Passing through.

He was passing—in sandals, woven poncho, jeans, silver bracelets, and finger cymbals—through the artificial wilderness that someone at the party had told him was called Central Park because it lay in the mindless middle of the whore called New York City. Her pimps—General Motors, Chase Manhattan. "How goes the war, General?" He and the general talked earnestly and imaginatively of chrome and horsepower while Chase Manhattan woke and winked in a Draculean vault and spat out shining untouched coins through a cracked front tooth.

He used the finger cymbals Gloria had given him, *click-clang,* and roused sleeping birds and the sun. The birds complained; the sun shuddered mournfully up the side of the Plaza Hotel.

Crinkled little paper cups that once had held smooth Italian ices in all the colors of every rainbow lay limp and empty on the grass around him. Ragged bits of potato chips eyed him anxiously as he crunched on. Dogs had been here before him. Their recent culinary history was everywhere, disguised. The ruins of Saturday's children skittered in the half-hearted wind—newspapers, soda straws, popcorn, scrawny peacock feathers, torn political posters. Saturday's children had fled hours before his advent, abandoning the park to the twisted and the reckless. Today was Sunday.

Click-clang. Softly, in deference to the early birds. A brass whimper, not a bang.

The terrestrial trees, he noticed, were glassy with leaves above his head as they flayed the empty sky with their strong branches in a brutal green silence he had never heard before.

There was a yellow balloon caught in one of the trees beneath which a shabbily clothed man lay snoring. Tock Von looked long at the yellow balloon, seeing a circus. He looked down at the man—an unemployed clown? He jumped up, caught the string tied around the puckered lip of the balloon, and ripped it free. He tied his finger cymbals to the string and then released the balloon. Some mysterious gas carried the globular rubber prison up to touch the sun, yellow on yellow. The tender eloquence of the ascending *click-clanging* woke the clown who muffled up against the tree. "Who're you?" he wheezed, obviously awaiting the inevitable roust or rolling.

"Prometheus," Tock Von replied, remembering his terrestrial mythology. He held out his wrists, flapped his hands limply. "My chains." The silver bracelets that had once belonged to a former novice jingled noncommittally.

"You plainclothes?"

"Looking like this?"

"They got 'em dressed up like girls over on the West Side. To catch the muggers. Like motorcycle nuts too. To catch the fags."

"You messed your clothes, man."

"That ain't none of your goddam business!"

"Take mine and welcome to them." Quickly, gaily—out of the poncho and off with the bracelets, kicking off sandals, dropping jeans and jockey shorts in an ecstasy of liberating and typical Eleisonite benignity.

The grizzled bear beneath the tree, totally unclowned now, grew canny. "You mean it, bo?"

Naked, nude, unclothed, bare-assed, vulnerable to the whimsy of the wind and the wet games of a not-yet rain. "Take them." And he was off on his erratic way beneath the trees which whispered secretly among themselves of orgasmic sap, above fingers of grass which groaned only to his ears as his bare toes pressed them down and down, within the rocking ocean of Earth's filthy air to which he was gradually becoming, a bit, accustomed.

Turning, turning, arms outstretched, giggling, genitals jiggling merrily, Tock Von watched the bearish clown in the woven poncho flap his scarecrow way toward a different destiny.

On.

Past benches and rocks, statues perched ponderously on fat pedestals—stone poets, a gilded dog, a mother in a pointed hat with a skinny goose at her cloaked side, an immense and grotesque Alice seated on a bronze toadstool—oh, the wonder of this new world.

On!

The cops were cooping.

The signs were raging:

DON'T LITTER.

NO LOITERING.

BICYCLISTS MUST FOLLOW MARKED PATHS.

DON'T . . . NO . . . STOP.

Needing no notebook, requiring no sheepskin or other encumbering academic paraphernalia, he glided on, planning on getting it all together—on cataloging and recording the facts, the figures, the shenanigans of the relatively hairless, relatively homicidal sapiens species that loped and lumbered along, together with fireflies and copperheads and eagles, giving the world a whirl for their three score and ten. Although for some, he would in time discover, a summer was all (twelve weeks of seeking sex and dodging fly swatters).

He found the zoo. And more signs. *Felis Leo*. Et cetera. He climbed over the guard rail and gripped the bars of a cage with both hands and spoke in all seriousness to the civet cat inside. They talked at length about the psychology of voyeurism and the merits of biped and quadruped nudity but they came in the end to no firm conclusion.

The keeper who first spotted Tock Von dropped his pail of corn cobs and held onto the guard rail for support. "*Arughh!*" Tock Von moved menacingly toward him. "Give me your keys!" He rolled his spooky gray eyes and shook his mane of black and thickly curled hair that ambushed his ears.

"*Arughh!*"

He roared an arpeggio.

The keeper turned, ran.

After him!

The two together, each uniformed in his peculiar way, ran wild under the amazed eyes of sleepy tigers and ever-aroused spider monkeys. At the end of the hundred yard dash, the keeper surrendered and led the way to the monkey house. He nervously handed Tock Von the keys, all the while babbling and evidently wishing he could bar the door of his world against apparitions.

Tock Von padded away, pitter-pattered in his bare feet past all the iron bars and the desultory eyes of the inmates. He fitted keys, fumbled about. Out leaped a lioness blinking golden in the sun. Raccoons minced free, their noses and tails twitching.

The humans, Tock Von noticed, were coming to the park now, unaware as yet that this would not be just another Sun Day of hangovers beside the seal pond while their children screeched and their heads rumbled, of wistful stares at unapproachable potential partners—oh, where did I go wrong?

He watched the monkeys masturbating in cool unconcern. He saw the women wearing girdles that pinched their increasing circumferences, watched them buying balloons. He sensed their indiscriminate hatred that made masks of their faces.

Under the Delacorte clock, which was always out of order, he watched them all parade without direction for the sake of the children. Alcoholic cotton, he knew, was stuck in the slick mouths of the angular New York girls who swung their hips in sad and ersatz freedom. In a small crowd in the distance, he noted the button-down male lips split at the seams as the Dutch organ played; and stocky women in wooden shoes and white caps who lived in Brooklyn sold souvenirs, and nobody thought to ask of what or why. Little boys in woolen shorts sat bored in the cart that the Shetland pony pulled as it shit its way around the track.

"Jay-*sus!*" roared a barrel-bellied subway conductor as he came knee to nose with a dislocated coyote. "Jay-*sus*, Mary, and Joseph! What the fuck?"

All the others were twisting out of the paths of pumas. Careening crazily, they ran, collided, recovered, ran again. Someone gave a scream that would intimidate the most vociferous parrot's talent. Chaos had come to the artificial jungle because bars had become unreliable and nothing was any longer predictable or dependable. It might as well have been Monday morning, six A.M., when clocks alarmed and frightened away every dream.

Busier than the most industrious beaver, Tock Von whistled happily at his work. He was confident of his goal. The people who had seen him preferred the company of the lions, unable to love a naked man in the wrong place at the wrong time. The gaudier girls peeped and purred to themselves in secret as they fled. ("He's not a bit bad-looking.") Matrons grew ripe with a rich scorn as they barricaded themselves in the cafeteria. Men roared their anger born of envy over their enemy's large attributes and demanded loudly that something be done.

He seized a girl in a red dress and locked her in an empty cage, accusing her of bearing obviously mercenary bedsores on her back. A man—lonely around the eyes and pockets—was next, accused of cheating on his income tax. He imprisoned eleven people of assorted sizes, shapes, and genders but all of the same species.

The manager of the cafeteria, behind the glass walls of his life, worried about the effect of all this on the day's business. He phoned the fuzz at the Park precinct and then hung up, smirking, satisfied.

It took no longer than usual, not quite forever, for them to come on their puttering scooters and snorting horny horses. The flags pasted on their windshields and bridles glared righteous red, white, and blue glances. Rabid mathematicians all, they quickly multiplied the confusion and added their own measure of alarm to what one outraged Indonesian diplomat from the United Nations tentatively designated "an untenable situation."

Tock Von climbed a tree as the fuzz came stumbling up in their aquamarine riot helmets and conscientious savagery. Up he went and up to perch on a limb high above the helmets held to lawful heads by sleek leather chin straps.

Voices bounced out from beneath the bobbing baby blue helmets:

"A goddam lily waver!"

"Mace him!"

"Call the ASPCA!"

Tock Von yodeled an Eleisonite answer in three-quarter time as he surveyed the scene with extraterrestrial detachment, his voice an Alpine iceberg. "Power to the panthers!" he called down to the city soldiers. "Free *Felis Leo.*"

"Free your ass!" a recruit responded cryptically.

A grandfatherly man took off his helmet and held it cupped against his chest as if he were trying to prevent his heart from popping out of its fleshy prison. He stared up into the tree and clucked a cock-of-the-walk tune. "What's your name, buddy?"

"Tock Von. What's yours?"

"Devlin. Al Devlin. Now, son, do you want to tell me what you did with your clothes?"

"I met a man who obviously needed them more than I did, so I gave them to him. You see, I've been taught that—"

"A psycho, Al," a blue colleague muttered confidentially.

From Al, "Where are the keys, friend? We've got to let those people out of the cages."

"Why?" With no sophistry or minced words.

"Why? Because they don't belong there, that's why!"

"How do you know?"

"Because, goddam it, those cages are for *animals!*"

"Just so." Tock Von swung from a branch, holding on with all ten fingers, his toes curling. "Tell you what, Al. I'll trade you one of mine for one of yours."

"Can't say as how I get you."

"You let one of your animals out of your jail and I'll let one of my animals out of the zoo."

"That's different. Jails aren't the same thing. So c'mon for Chris' sake! Where the hell are the keys?"

"They've got this Serengeti Plain over in Africa. Like, you know, where the animals are left alone to do their own thing. Why don't you rip off a few blocks up in the Bronx, say, and stock it with your game and let them do *their* own thing? Cages aren't natural."

Devlin wiped the sweat from his forehead and turned away from the tree just as a man in a uniform darted past him with a rope net held in his outstretched hands. The man threw the net but missed the cockatoo he was aiming at. It flounced screeching up to the roof of the elephant house.

"Hey, you!" Devlin yelled and the man halted, turned.

"Yes, sir?"

The "sir" noticeably stiffened Devlin's spine. "You from the ASPCA?"

"Yes, sir. From the Shelter, sir. We were called. Because of all the animals—because—"

They talked and agreed. Yes, it could definitely be done. A bit unorthodox but then so was this Sunday morning.

Tock Von calmly watched them stretch the huge net beneath his tree. He saw the man in the uniform go and return with an odd gun cradled in his arms. He looked down at the command post the fuzz had established at a sufficiently safe distance from his tree and then up at the rising muzzle of the gun. He had a chilling moment of misgiving as he imagined crosshairs, himself frozen in their hairline juncture. But there were always risks involved in dealing with an alien species, he reminded himself. He was perfectly willing to take them. He rose up on his toes, gave Devlin a smart salute and waited for the drug dart to strike, planning on initiating peace talks later and presenting a persuasive argument for the reordering of certain earthly priorities.

Piffff!

Oooffff!

In the shoulder. They evidently don't want to damage the pelt, he thought. It just might be the style next season —Genuine Alienskin, $249.95 in the new kicky crotch length.

Already the drug was rippling through his arterial tributaries on its way to the turbulent ocean of his brain, confusing his corpuscles along the way. His limbic lobe was being lullabyed. He raised his arms, did a slow soft-shoe, shoeless, and swan-dived gracefully down into the waiting net, singing in lugubrious Eleisonite.

A photographer from the *Daily News* snapped and snickered as he immortalized it all for the lip-moving Monday morning millions, who always turned first to the paper's centerfold photos for their daily hype of arrested call girls wearing huge shades, and a man perched on the

Brooklyn Bridge while the people down below shouted, "*Jump!*"

Sin at a safe distance and somebody else's death, Tock Von thought as he slipped quickly into the net and sleep.

TWO

"Cheer, cheer for Eleison.
Onward, onward, through apogee!"

Tock Von was on the toilet.

The toilet was in Bellevue Hospital.

Bellevue Hospital was in New York City.

New York City was in the United States.

And so on up to the universe by means of basic spatial extrapolation, he thought, and then said, "They have bars on all the windows and doors."

A leathery Negro, too old and out of it to be called a "black," spit out a loose front tooth. "Keeps them out. Heh, heh."

His tooth lay oddly white on the dark tile floor. He wiped himself, pulled up his beltless, shapeless hospital pants. He looked sternly down into the bowl before flushing it with a theatrical flourish. "You are what you eat." *Whooossshhh!*

From the stool next to the Negro, Tock Von said, "They put pants on me. I wonder if they did the same for all the other animals."

Once back in the barren dayroom, he sat down on the

floor and began to count the bars. "—three, four, close the door . . ."

All around the almost totally chairless room, the patients stared and wandered. Carousing with demons that were private or dancing to tunes that only they could hear, they were unamused.

Tock Von listened to the conversation taking place between a wily-eyed young man with tattoos on his cheeks and a girl named Vivian, who wasn't there.

"So I goes," said Tattoos, " 'Like if you're gonna only bring a few lousy oranges as your share and then figure all the rest is yours, well, you ain't.' "

". . . . . ," said Vivian.

"So then he goes, 'It ain't right you should blame me for the heist. It was probably an addict that took your freak-ass radio.'

"So I goes, 'Yeah, and Charlie from the pawnshop over on Eighth Avenue who tole me what you did, he don't know you by sight even though you bring him what you rip off every day, huh?"

". . . . ."

"Shut up, Vivian. I ain't finished."

". . . . ."

"I said *shut up!* So then he goes, 'I'll tell you what. You want a radio? I'll get you a radio. One with a clock in it yet—from Macy's I'll lift it. Then we'll be square, right?'

" 'Wrong,' I goes. 'If you're gonna crash here, you gotta do more'n bring in a few moldy oranges. You gotta keep your hands off what's mine too and that includes Vivian!' "

". . . . . ," said Vivian.

"You're goddam right I told him!"

Tock Von returned to counting the bars which numbered twenty-eight if you didn't count the chicken wire covering the hole in the wall where they kept the television set. Twenty-eight bars plus walls formed the iron boundaries of the Bellevue ward, which was alive with loud as well as mute satellites unmoored within its starless space. He had met them all, more or less. . . .

Mr. Cardinal: "They say it has something to do with

my name, but it's really just that I *like* people to kiss my ring."

Ralph Cordoba: "They call me crazy just because I pissed in the street. Hell, dogs do it all the time."

A man who called himself simply A: "Act always as an aardvark and all apples are available afterward."

Plus the nameless man who ran an invisible liquor store by the window: "Gallo wine is all I sell, but I can see that you are a discriminating devotee of Bacchus, and I therefore offer you a special price on a case of muscatel. Thank you, sir. Gallo wine is all I sell, but I can see you are a discriminating devotee . . ."

All of them, Tock Von knew, were out of their heads, out to lunch where visions were the uniform of the day and where being crazy, crackers, cuckoo was the only game in their particular town at the time. The man sold his wine endlessly, and Bacchus frolicked vined in his greensward dreams. They were, Tock Von decided, the summer soldiers enlisted only for a season, but they were finding it hard to get a discharge. Some of them probably sensed, however dimly, that somewhere there were gentler fields waiting to be plowed and roof beams yearning to be raised before another awful winter came with snow on its stomping boots, and only cold in the empty cavity where its heart should have been. Carrying their invisible burdens, they were the stragglers in a contemporary crusade.

It was a season of goodby-saying in Bellevue, Tock Von realized. A time of unbinding. The cerements of civilization had come totally and perhaps irrevocably undone. Beyond the bars off-duty policemen shot men who insulted them, and judges knew more of accommodation than of justice, and a girl in Harlem figured what-the-hell and flopped down while the boys pounced with their cocks at the ready, suspecting sadly that making it might be all that mattered, besides which it paid the rent.

The old Negro had said it about the bars. "Keeps *them* out." Not an altogether bad bargain when there was Mr. Cardinal's death's head ring to be kissed and secret pipers in cellular dungeons who played it with crazed soul, played it cool. The fears that stalked the citizens of Bellevue were no worse, Tock Von suspected, because of his previous research, than those that were alive in the halls of ivy or in Danbury, Connecticut.

The attendant at the door turned and called out, "Hey, you!" He pointed the hairy finger of God.

But Adam did not awaken.

The attendant lumbered over, bent down, reached under Tock Von's arms and lifted.

"My name is Tock Von."

"Sure, baby. Sure thing."

Baby, alias Tock Von, was dragged to the door and pushed through it into the arms of another attendant who promptly and deftly cracked baby's shin with the aluminum clipboard he carried in his manicured hand.

"That's better, kid. I knew you could walk by yourself."

Tock Von put one foot forward and then the other. Down the corridor he went toward another door. Whistling? No. Sucking sustenance from the air. It only sounded like whistling. Anyway it wasn't dark. Locks. Keys. Locks. Keys.

"Good morning, Doctor Krizwinkle," crooned the attendant as he shoved Tock Von into a dingy office.

"Good morning, Jerry," Krizwinkle said. To Tock Von, he said, "Come in. Sit down over there."

"That man—Jerry," Tock Von began once he was seated.

"Yes?"

"He hit me on the shin with his clipboard. It really wasn't necessary, you know. He seemed to be expecting resistance, but I've visited Earth often enough to know that resistance is essentially impossible, not to mention unwise."

"Have people hit you often, in your opinion?"

"No. Now and then. But not exactly what you could call often." Tock Von wondered how he could put the doctor at ease, how to stop his rabbity twitching. "You have a very nice office here."

"The people who hit you? Who are they?"

"Fuzz mostly. The Man. On one of my recent trips, I marched in a peace demonstration. With a club."

"You took a club to a peace demonstration?"

"No. The fuzz took theirs."

"You feel then that people pick on you."

"When I tell them who I am."

"Do you know who you are?"

"Sure. I'm Tock Von from—"

"Do you hear voices?"

"All the time."

"Can you describe them?"

"Well, yours, I'd say, is pleasant enough. Maybe a little bit nasal."

"That isn't what I meant. Do you like girls?"

"Guys too."

"I see. Do you know where you are?"

"On Earth."

"This is Bellevue Hospital and you are a patient here. You were arrested yesterday in Central Park for indecent exposure among other things. What day is this—do you know?"

It was getting uncomfortable. Tock Von sensed that the doctor felt it too—he was fidgeting with his horn rims.

"Please take a look at this card and tell me what you see."

Tock Von took the card. "Those are rondys. Red and purple rondys."

"Rondys?" The doctor's eyebrows elevated.

"They grow on the crystalline ronds when our suns are at Eleison-D."

"And this one?" Doctor Krizwinkle offered Tock Von a second card.

"A non-linear representation of our National Anthem."

"Can you sing it for me?"

Tock Von cleared his throat. "Cheer, cheer for Eleison. Onward, onward, through apogee . . ."

"Thank you, that is quite enough. This one? Can you make up a story to go with this picture?"

"The girl who's pushing the Good Humor cart fought for equal rights for women, so they hired her, but they gave her a route in the slums. Revenge for her agitation, sort of. It's torn her heart out. Having heard about the girl's torn-out heart, the Aztec priest filed for property rights to her heart on a tax-exempt basis, claiming a non-profit religious foundation as the beneficiary. He—"

"Where do you see the Aztec priest in the picture?"

"I don't. He's not because they disallowed his claim."

"The Good Humor cart?"

"Parked out of sight in an alley off 125th Street."

"And the girl?"

"In the hospital for a transplant operation." Tock Von handed back the picture of a meadow which stretched prone under a gloomy sky.

"We'll talk some more another time," Doctor Krizwinkle said. And sighed.

A boy was lying in the middle of the dayroom floor, crying. It was, Tock Von thought, a rather musical sound, a loud aria needing only a bullring, and the shouts of an offstage crowd, and some stirring music to turn it into art.

Tock Von was sitting beside him, stroking his shoulder and ignoring the cries of "cocksucker" from some of the watching patients. The boy's hair was almost white and his cheeks were fat pouches above his pale lips. His tears made salty puddles on the floor. The attendant guarding the locked door gnawed his nails in silence as he looked away to happier horizons.

As Tock Von stroked the boy's shoulder sympathetically, the salty rain at last ended.

"I've never been in a place like this before," moaned the boy without lifting his forehead from the floor. "I never expected."

Tock Von continued to gently stroke the boy's shoulder. What was there to say? Call the fire department —my house is on fire and my brain burns? No good. He kept on stroking in a steady down-time rhythm.

"It happened to me," said the boy, "in a movie theater. I thought the people were coming right out of the screen after me. I started screaming. I was so *scared!*"

I was so scared! Words to die by. Nobody knows the trouble I've seen. . . . And all the others . . . Tock Von remembered other human beings he had encountered on other earlier field trips. . . .

The woman in the supermarket with her over-loaded shopping cart trundling down the aisles wearing rolled-over white anklets and gray molded shoes. Hair in enormous curlers beneath a fuchsia scarf: *Souvenir of Miami Beach.* Picking up cans, bottles, boxes, jars—checking prices, comparing the weights of Brand X with Brand Y. Taking two, three at a time. *Buy!* Stock the larder! Famine is abroad in the land, and Hunger of Heart is the new Number One Killer in America. Pickles in 57 varieties, potato chips in whispering cellophane, TV dinners as frozen as plastic roses, cheese Danish, six cans of beer, juicy grapefruit, minute rice, peas, cereals that snap, crackle, and snarl, sweet potatoes, watermelon, cashews.

Don't cry.

The man with the mustache and muscles in the Old Erin Bar and Grille standing with his foot on the brass rail and ordering up. "Yo!" to the bartender wiping up beer. "I'll have me another boilermaker, bud." Call him "bud." Make friends. Get along. Pay your way. Smile. Somebody elbowing in, a foreigner by the greasy looks of him. Cracking jokes about nuns and niggers. Mustache and muscles beginning to bristle. Insisting, "My mother was a saint!" And, "Your mother eats it, ace!" Fists. Flying glass. And the fury that was another name for fear. An ambulance. A few stitches and off to a bored cashier to pay for the catgut. What if she wasn't? Wasn't a saint? Wasn't? Oh!

Don't cry.

The girl in the subway. After midnight. Deserted platform. Gum machines that don't work and trash all around. Edging away, looking back over her shoulder hopefully. Thinking: *Oh, please, God, make the train come quick! No one will hear me scream. He has such spooky gray eyes. Is this all? To die of a switch-blade and terror in this dingy Bowling Green subway station?* Nervous. Pretty. Young. Always in season. Too bad. "Don't, mister, please. Don't hurt me." What's her name? "Peaches." Let it go, let it ride. "You're going to hurt me." Telling her, "I'm not, honest." "You are." The train coming at last and her not getting hurt like she wanted. What's a nice masochist like you doing in a place like this?

"Don't cry," Tock Von said to the shuddering boy on the floor.

"Okay."

"See the attendant over there? He's dreaming of getting a better job—civil service is safe—maybe as a mailman. Something respectable anyway. You know, the nuts in here get to a guy after a while, and there's the wife and the kid on the way to consider. A man's got to look out for the future. They say being crazy might even be contagious!"

The boy laughed at last. "You're okay at least."

"I hope."

"I'm going to get better."

"Give 'em hell!"

And then once again, the selective finger of God pointing. "Hey, you!"

"Me?" Tock Von inquired innocently.

"Yeah, you. The doctor wants to see you."

"Why?"

"Forget the questions. Just get it up, okay? Get it *up!*"

Tock Von got it quickly up.

"Come in," said Doctor Krizwinkle, beckoning to Tock Von. "Sit down please. Thank you, Jerry. You can wait right outside."

Who was the other guy in the room besides Krizwinkle—the one with the tinted shades, Tock Von wondered. He was a small man, a fat man, and he beamed behind his green tinted glasses. His head was bald. He smiled and smiled.

Tock Von smiled back.

"This gentleman is Doctor Everest Quest," declared Krizwinkle. "He very much wanted to meet you."

"How do you do, young man?" said Doctor Quest.

"I do okay considering," Tock Von replied.

"Considering?" Quest raised an expectant eyebrow.

"Considering the fact that the courses I took in human history and cultural affairs couldn't possibly provide me with all the information I evidently need to get along here on Earth."

"You are a college student then, I take it? Your courses, I gather, are less than satisfactory to you?"

Tock Von somewhat wearily explained to Quest what he meant.

"So you're an alien," Quest commented when Tock Von had completed his careful explanation.

"Right on," Tock Von declared experimentally, vaguely uneasy in the modern idiom of the young. "On the other hand, however," he quickly added, "*you* are the alien. You and all other humans. From my point of view, that is."

"Of course," Quest agreed. He turned to Krizwinkle. "Fritz, his delusions have the perfect interior consistency of the paranoiac. Do you remember the patient we interviewed years ago when we were residents together? The one with the massive persecution complex? Remember how he insisted that people were writing things about him in the newspaper?"

Krizwinkle giggled. "When we pointed out to him that the papers were actually writing about Hitler and Hirohito, he simply insisted that the reporters had changed the names in an attempt to confuse him. But the articles, he maintained, were actually about him."

Quest clasped his ringed hands over his paunch. "Such fantastic consistency is a characteristic of the illness, of course. But its logic within the weird framework of the aberration continually amazes me. As it does in this young man's case."

Tock Von glanced at the door. Closed. Bars on the windows.

Quest said, "Tock Von, I'd like to ask you a question if I may. What is your real name?"

Tock Von told him.

Quest glanced meaningfully at Krizwinkle. "Your address?"

"The Planet Eleison in the Sixteenth Star System of the Gamma Galaxy."

"Did you use acid?" Quest inquired.

"No. But a drug trip is scheduled. We're going to a commune in Oklahoma on our next—my seventh field trip."

Quest was shaking his head. "No, you misunderstand me. What I meant was, how did you manage to eliminate your fingerprints? Acid has been used by some criminals to achieve that end."

"We never bothered with minor details," Tock Von explained. "Fingerprints weren't really necessary. We could pass as humans if the general conformation, the clearly visible parts, were correct and functional."

"Everything else about you seems to be normal," Quest mused, glaring at Tock Von, "based on the tests we've made. Blood constituency, bone structure, internal organs, metabolism. But no fingerprints. Not a one."

"That should support the truth of what I've been telling you," Tock Von pointed out. "I mean that I really am not human. '

"It's quite true," Quest continued, "that fingerprints can be partially destroyed but no case is known in which all—I repeat, all—configurations have been eliminated. But your prints have been completely obliterated."

"They have not been! I mean they were never created in the first place!"

"Doctor Quest," said Krizwinkle, "has a proposal to make to you—uh, Tock Von."

"Yes, I have," said Quest quickly. "I have an establishment—a residence, let's call it—where selected patients such as yourself can be cured of the delusions that hamper their lives. It is called Excelsior and it is located on the bank of the Hudson River in a perfectly lovely area. Scenic, you know. I would happily welcome you as a guest."

"You humans charge money to stay at an establishment like you mentioned, right?"

"An exception will be made in your case," Quest said. "To be perfectly frank with you, yours is a most interesting case. We have had patients in the past, of course, who have thought of themselves as key figures in history—Napoleon, Mussolini—but I've never encountered a sick person before who actually believed he was from another planet. But times change, don't they? Well. Your cure would benefit Excelsior immensely. We would have more applicants for admittance than we could possibly handle. It would give us a chance to be of wide-reaching service to all the ill and psychically injured who would seek us out as a result of your cure which we would, of course, publicize thoroughly."

"No, thank you," Tock Von said. "I've got things to do here on Earth, things to see. Sorry."

Quest looked at Krizwinkle. Krizwinkle looked at the door.

"We checked the Missing Persons Bureau," Quest said to Krizwinkle, ignoring Tock Von. "They have no record of him. If he vanished, no one would miss him."

"Jerry!" Krizwinkle called out.

The door opened.

Tock Von raced toward it.

Past the midget gorilla named Jerry, he ran. Prince Kong made a grab for him. Missed.

Out in the corridor, nurses began scurrying out of the way. One looked twelve years old and starched out of her wits. She didn't scurry. She fainted.

Prince Kong grunted down the corridor in cold pursuit of Tock Von.

Tock Von leaped up and grabbed the chicken wire covering the overhead light fixture. As Prince Kong came toward him, he swung both feet. Prince Kong grabbed one ankle and held on.

Tock Von found himself on the floor.

Quest and Krizwinkle came hurrying down the corridor toward them. Prince Kong knew what to do until the doctor came. A swift surreptitious blow to Tock Von's vulnerable balls.

"Ooooooo!"

Quest arrived and said, "A most magnificent opportunity."

"The end, Everest," Krizwinkle said solemnly, "justifies the medicinal means."

"Let him stay here a few days," Quest suggested. "Take down his history as he understands it. I'd appreciate it,

Fritz." He gripped his colleague's arm. "Excelsior Common is doing quite fantastically well over the counter. I'll see to it that you receive another hundred shares within the week."

"Jerry," said Krizwinkle, "take Tock Von back to the ward."

Rocked in the cradle of Prince Kong's arms, Tock Von tried to figure out why everything seemed to be going so suddenly and so thoroughly wrong.

THREE

"Watch it, Goliath.
I'm a slingshot freak."

The doctors at Bellevue Hospital listened politely to Tock Von in the days and interviews that followed. They duly noted in his growing file the name of his home planet and the incredible story he told of his genesis. They made obscure notes and nodded wisely to one another. They viewed most of his facts concerning Eleison with the same jaded distaste as that which they gave to the other patients' chronic complaints concerning the flies that had infiltrated the walls, the FBI microphones hidden in the hospital spoons, the electrified urinals, and similar gaudy aberrations.

Tock Von did not despair.

Instead, he made lists:

1. Ku Klux Klan, dum-dum bullets, anti-perspirants, multiple sclerosis telethons, My Lai, ABM, IBM, supersonic jet transports, zoos, hunting licenses, Disneyland, electric chairs, Barby dolls.
2. Santa Claus, Eleison, fairies.
3. charles manson, kate smith, elijah muhammed,

george lincoln rockwell, francis cardinal spellman, richard speck, shirley temple, julius hoffman, mickey mouse, andy warhol, bull connor, billy graham, eric sevareid, howdy doody.

With his pencil held between his teeth, he looked at his lovely lists. He would send them to his doctor. He began to write suitable headings for each list:

1. Anthropoid atrocities.
2. Facts.
3. Noted Americans, past and present.

He went up to the new attendant who was standing rigidly against the door, evidently expecting to be torn limb from innocent limb by the crazies at any inauspicious minute. "Take this to your leader, man, okay?"

"What is it?"

"It's a secret message. He might understand."

"Who?"

"The doctor."

"Oh."

"It's a message from the front. Tell him that the battle still rages and although the men are weary, Captain, their morale remains high. Quick! Before the rocket's red glare fades and your flag is not there!"

Doctor (a Tock Vonian fantasy) takes the message, reads it, and promptly slays the messenger who brings such bad news. An American tragedy.

Tock Von headed back to the melee of djinns on the rampage and shouted an encouraging SHAZAM! which had no effect at all on him or on the djinns.

In the country of the blind, Tock Von thought later that same day, the one-eyed man was king. In the land of the one-eyed men, Cyclops was just another citizen. Logic. Such were his thoughts as Prince Kong reappeared with cohorts by his side, including a nurse, a straitjacket lying limp in his huge hands.

Tock Von gave the mélange no resistance. The attendants held him down on the floor and the nurse injected the hypodermic needle.

"What's in it?" he asked her, not wanting to waste an opportunity for earthly self-education.

"Sodium amytal," the ogress replied. "Start counting backward from ten."

"—nine, eight, seven—"

In the buzzing haze rising around him, Tock Von suddenly saw the crimson foliage of the trees of Eleison. He remembered the rich white wind that swept its lovely way through the elevated cities. He felt a yearning within him—a weak cry of yearning for the known and familiar. But all that would have to wait until . . .

Meanwhile, in the thick fog surrounding him, he caught a glimpse of the streams and rivers of Eleison, glittering golden as they rippled their rampant way to iridescent seas.

He awoke sometime later in the ambulance roaring its way up the Henry Hudson Parkway. Looking out the window from the stretcher to which he was tightly strapped, he saw the Hudson River pulsing polluted to the sea and the gull-begrimed Statue of Liberty in her steel skirt and motto. *Give me your tired, your poor, your troubled masses yearning to breathe free.* Free, he thought on several levels. Free of straitjackets, and free too of mortgages, and instant coffee, and General Electric, and commuter trains, and fivermotherfuckingpercent at the local Savings and Loan, and the albatross of dead dreams.

He watched the trees flick past, heavy with birds and bark. He caught glimpses of the houses of the well-to-do perched on the banks of the Hudson, and he thought of quaint Swiss clocks striking all the empty hours, bears popping out, burdened with briefcases. Women with brooms twirling and sweeping, sweeping and twirling, on their mechanical track while their wombs withered beneath expensive silk. Another day, another disaster.

A church pointed an accusing steeple at the sky and then was gone in a rush of wind past the technological chariot in which he was riding. Look at all the human kids, he thought, coming home from school where they have been taught that only their corrupt Congress can declare war and other lies just as atrocious.

After a time, the ambulance slowed and then parked beside an opaque geodesic dome somewhere north of Riverdale. The driver and his helper got out and unloaded the stretcher and its burden.

Tock Von stared up in awe at the gleaming architectural marvel. *Sweet J. C. it was Big Rock Candy Mountain!*

The dome seemed to be made of a single unseamed piece of opaque glass, or perhaps it was plastic. Its circumference was vast. It had no visible doors.

Beeep!

Following the mellow tone, a gelded male voice crooned, "Welcome to Excelsior. When you hear the next tone, please state your name first and your reason for coming here second."

Beeep!

An attendant: "My name's Frank and my buddy here is Eddie. We brought you guys a psycho case name of Tock Von."

"One moment please."

Hey now, Tock Von marveled. Will you take a look at the Lost City of the Insane! Not on any known map! And, wow! The glass egg was decapitating itself!

He watched a portion of the top of the dome slowly rise. A trapdoor? This way to the egress?

Suddenly there was a whirring of wings as an enormous red helicopter emerged from the open dome. It fluttered down loudly to land nearby on the asphalt driveway, its blades gradually shuddering themselves to silence.

Beeep!

"The patient will board the helicopter please, assuming he is ambulatory."

Frank and Eddie looked at one another, shrugged, and unbound the straps and then the straitjacket.

"You heard the man," Eddie said to Tock Von.

Tock Von, feeling a little giddy, hauled himself up into the helicopter.

Beeep!

"Make yourself comfortable, sir. The helicopter is radio controlled. In a moment, you will be flying."

In a moment he was flying through the air with the greatest of ease. He marveled at the many seats. Enough, he estimated, to accommodate the entire Mormon Tabernacle Choir. Red leather seats. Buttery soft and expensive. He was floating noisily down through the dome's aperture, which closed behind him. The helicopter landed on the roof of one of the pistachio buildings that squatted in the center of the tutti-frutti complex.

A door opened in the little round turret on top of the building, and a man in an immaculate white suit strode toward Tock Von as he eased himself down from the helicopter.

"How do you do? My name is Pomeroy."

Tock Von obligingly took the offered hamhock hand. He was, he admitted to himself, somewhat in awe of Pomeroy's rogue elephant shoulders and his tiny eyes of amber. He shook the hamhock hand and came away with five flattened fingers.

"This way," said Pomeroy, escorting Tock Von to the steel elevator that lay just beyond the door in the turret. "Doctor Quest is waiting for you in his office."

Tock Von, anticipating screams and other unnerving events, was surprised when the elevator stopped and a calm young girl got on. She had brown hair that glistened as it crept below her shoulders. She had the face of a stunning Japanese geisha translated into understandable American terms—smooth skin, silken eyes, rounded cheekbones like gentle barricades.

He spoke to her. "Hi, there. My name's Tock Von."

She gave him a small smile, suitably inscrutable.

"Do you—uh, live here?" he inquired carefully, not wanting to hurt her feelings.

"They say I'm crazy, if that's what you mean." She stepped off the elevator when it stopped on the main floor and disappeared around a bend in the corridor.

Pomeroy said, "The doctor's office is just down the hall."

"Who did the paintings on the wall over there? Some of your more disturbed patients?"

"They're French Impressionists. Doctor Quest is an art collector among many other things."

"Well, I don't know anything about art but I know what I don't like," Tock Von commented, unimpressed by the French.

Entering Quest's office, Tock Von found, was a kind of shock therapy. Purple damask drapes hung on the windows. The walls were paneled in oak. There was indirect lighting and a walnut desk that spanned one entire end of the room. Carpet all over—it was like walking on sponges.

Doctor Quest rose from behind his desk and came around it to greet Tock Von. "Ah, here we are, aren't we?" he declared jovially. "Sit down, do. Anywhere at all. We're quite informal here. An unstructured environment, we've found, is best for our therapeutic purposes. Now then, young man."

"Watch it, Goliath. I'm a slingshot freak."

"Oh ho, ho, ho!" Quest clasped his hands over his stomach as he sat down again across from his guest, as he called Tock Von. He began at once to describe his establishment. "We have entertainments—musicales, country fairs, dances—all sorts of wonderful things. Excelsior is an almost completely self-sufficient unit. We have our own laundry, our own gardens, organic, in which we grow nutritious foods. We slaughter our own animals. A generator provides us with electricity. We are connected to the local water supply and sewage system, of course. Unfortunately, one cannot be totally independent in today's complex world. But, all in all, we do quite well for and by ourselves. Now that we meet again, let me ask you once more if you can tell me who you are exactly."

"Exactly?"

"Try, do."

"I am Tock Von from the planet Eleison in the Sixteenth Star System of the Gamma Galaxy."

"How very interesting, um. And you came here, I assume, by space ship?"

"No. Two guys drove me."

"I mean you came to Earth in a space ship."

"No, not like that. It was a different kind of trip entirely. You wouldn't understand."

"You say your name is Tock Von?"

"I say."

"We'll have to do something about that name. Yes, something. Tock Von. Von Tock. No. But yes, still something." Musing, Quest steepled his fingers under his chins.

"Doc," Tock Von ventured, "I met a girl in the elevator. Tall. Sexy. What's her problem?"

"You must mean Monica Seaver. A most interesting case, yes indeed. Monica had a baby."

"It happens all the time."

"Not quite as it happened this time, at least not according to Monica. Hers, you see, was a virgin birth. Or so she tells us."

"Well, there is a precedent in your human history."

"A gynecological examination contradicted Monica's claim."

"So you locked her up here."

"She is our guest, yes. Now then, Tock Von, perhaps you'd be good enough to fill out this form for me. Don't ponder too much over the questions. Just put down whatever first occurs to you. Spontaneity often gives us clues to the subconscious. I'll leave you alone for a few minutes. I shall return shortly."

When Quest had gone, Tock Von picked up the form he had been given and began to fill it out.

Name *Tock Von* Marital Status *None*

Address *Planet Eleison*

Date of birth *Starday Six*

List any serious illnesses you have had *War*

Fill in the spaces with words beginning with the following letters:

J*udas* D*rug* F*ree* E*nterprise*

If you could have three wishes, what would they be? (List in order of preference.)

1 To ball today

2 To ball tomorrow

3 To ball the day after tomorrow

Do you have Major Medical Insurance? .... Yes ✓ .... No

Religion Refuse to answer on grounds it may incriminate me.

Name of person to be notified in case of emergency Monica Seaver

Place a check next to the statement which best describes you:

✓ I am happy ✓ I am angry ✓ I am dangerous

✓ I am lonely ✓ I am beautiful ✓ I am truthful

Place a check next to the name of the person you would most like to resemble:

...... Babe Ruth ...... Golda Meir ...... Captain Hook

...... Marilyn Monroe ...... Sidney Poitier ...... Queen Victoria

...... King Farouk ...... Peter Pan ✓ Jesus Christ

Signed Tock Von

He dropped the form on the desk and went to the door which he quickly discovered had no knob. How to open it? He fiddled with it to no avail. He pounded on it. Nothing. He kicked it. Nothing.

He sat down and propped his feet on the desk. He took a cigar from Quest's glass humidor and lit it.

He didn't hear the door open behind him. But at the sound of footsteps shushing through the swamp of the carpet, he turned.

"Ah, I see you've made yourself quite comfortable," Quest observed. "That's fine." He blubbered his way around behind his desk and sat down. "Ah, and you've finished filling out our little form. Good. Let us have a look. Very interesting. So you would like to resemble Jesus Christ, um?"

"Um, yes."

"May I ask why?"

"Sure."

A pause and then an irritated, "Well, why?"

"So I could consort freely and openly with prostitutes without getting busted."

"And yet I notice that you refuse to list your religion."

"Jesus Christ has nothing to do with religion. That's a contradiction in terms."

"Um."

"Tell me something, Doc."

"If I can."

"How'd you get that knob-less door open?"

"They are one of our innovations, the doors. They respond electronically to retinal pattern recognition. No keys are needed. We'll encode your pattern and then you'll be free to come and go as you please in most areas of our establishment. Your room, the grounds. But not the Arena, of course."

"The Arena?"

"The Arena." Quest grinned from jowl to jowl. "You'll be paying a visit to the Arena quite soon. It is the central element in our treatment program. A bit unorthodox perhaps but effective."

"Tell me about this treatment program of yours." The guy's crazy, Tock Von thought. He grins like a collie.

"To begin with, let me say that people who become mentally ill have simply closed their eyes to the way the real world works. Which, of course, brings us at once to fantasy. Now fantasy is fine in its proper place, I admit. But fantasy unchecked—fantasy run wild, so to speak—ah, now that is something else. Fantasy is the source of art, of course, as we all know. But it is also—or it can be—a source of aberration. Because it contradicts reality. Channeling it, we have found, does little good. Channeling fantasy does little more than produce hypertense military men and second-rate poets. What we teach here is reality.

Reality!" Quest tasted the word, tongued it as if it were a lush, ripe cherry. "We teach our patients how to accept and cope with reality. Indeed, how to use it to their own best advantage. We change minds here. Oh ho, ho, ho! Literally, if you take my meaning."

"I'm trying."

"Think back to the Crusades. The Crusaders tried to change people's minds. They did it with swords and lances. Inefficient. The Inquisition also tried to change people's minds. The Inquisitors did it with iron maidens and the rack. They achieved only partial and temporary success. Too many relapses once their subjects were released. Well, I'm sure you see what I mean. There are no whips or chains here. No iron boots or branding irons. We work in more positive and productive ways. We place our patients in an educational situation and we motivate them to learn by a simple system of rewards and punishments."

"Punishments? Man, I thought you said—"

Quest held up a hand. "No need for alarm. We punish by withdrawing our love and approval from patients who prove poorly motivated. We reward them, however, with tenderness and concern. Once you have spent some little time with us, you will experience how well our system works. Tock Von, I will tell you a truth. All our patients want desperately to be loved as I am certain you do. The more they want love, the more willing and, I might add, able they are to learn within our system. The Arena is our operating room, in a sense, as you shall soon see. It is our laboratory. Our nursery school."

He sounds full of shit up to his eyeballs, Tock Von decided.

"We are builders here. But we are also a demolition team." Steel struck sparks in Quest's large eyes behind their tinted green glasses. "We break down delusions. Our wrecking ball swings and useless illusions crumble to dust. Then we move in with our lathes and our lumber, and we build new men and new women. You shall see."

"I'm okay the way I am."

"You're not. You don't fit into—ah, human society. Did you not yourself say and insist that you were an alien?

But you will fit." Quest leaned across his desk and whispered in a snake's voice, "To begin with—your name. I've been thinking anagrammatically about it. To make it more suitable to your present—uh, earthly circumstances, a rearrangement of the letters would seem to be in order. Novotck. Now how does that strike you?"

"I like my name the way it is."

"Well, if you insist. But you'll soon develop a more cooperative and realistic attitude. I guarantee it."

Tock Von suppressed an involuntary shiver as he sensed the Questian wrecking ball swinging eagerly toward the thin walls of his skull.

FOUR

"What what is is the the Arena Arena?"

The window in the room to which he was assigned, Tock Von quickly discovered, was not a normal window. It was made of glass, but there its resemblance to any other window he had ever looked through on Earth ended. This window, the one with the smooth surface and faintly yellow patina, did not look out on the grounds of Excelsior. Tock Von found that by pressing a button in the sill, the window would show him vistas.

Press—a moonscape.

Press—a pastoral scene complete with nymphs and satyrs.

The room possessed other amenities as well. Lying on his bed, Tock Von felt invisible fingers massage his muscles. A certain tricky turn to the left of the faucet on the sink in the room brought not hot and not cold water but ginger ale. The walls were soft. So were the floors. Tock Von began to feel like a seed in some strangely sprouting fruit. A worm? On occasion.

Within an hour after having been assigned to the room, he greeted Pomeroy as the man appeared with no sound or fanfare, a kit in his hands. When he had connected wires to the dial on the mechanism which the kit contained, he said to Tock Von, "Open wide."

Tock Von opened his mouth.

Pomeroy patiently shook his head. "Your eyes, please."

Tock Von closed his mouth and opened his eyes wide.

"Blink, please."

Tock Von obliged.

"We will program your retinal pattern into the door system," Pomeroy promised. "You will then be free to come and go here and there."

"How long will it take you?"

"Not long."

It didn't take long. Half an hour later, when Tock Von, eyed like an eagle, blinked at his door, it opened and he went through it.

He wandered alone down the corridor, blinking at every door he encountered. All opened. All save the largest one on the main floor.

"That, young man," chirped a thrush of a woman as she hopped up to Tock Von, "is the door leading to the Arena. None of us can open it, no matter how furiously or conscientiously we blink at it."

"What's the Arena exactly?" Tock Von inquired as he walked along with the old woman whose hair was the color of ice and whose busy body seemed incapable of stillness.

"I'm Miss Dear," the woman volunteered, ignoring the question. "Why, you can't be more than ten years old, young man."

"I'm twice that," Tock Von responded. "That is, as you humans measure time."

"Well, never mind," said Miss Dear. "No need to apologize. Absolutely no need. You see, when you get to be my age, why, everyone looks so terribly *young!* That's because I'm seventy-five years old—seventy-six come next April. Just what did you mean by that remark about the way we humans measure time?"

Tock Von hesitated and then decided to plunge forward. "I'm not human, Miss Dear. I'm what you would call an alien. From another planet."

"Well, it takes all kinds," Miss Dear commented vaguely. Then, glancing up and down the empty corridor, she leaned close to Tock Von, took his arm, and whispered in the voice of a restrained whirlwind, "Have you seen any of them yet?"

"Seen any of who?"

"Them!" Miss Dear stared up at Tock Von in surprise. She released his arm and quickly wiped her hands on her black crepe dress. "I shouldn't have said anything. Why you might even be one of them!"

"One of who?" Tock Von, like Miss Dear, glanced uneasily up and down the empty corridor.

"Do you have credentials, young man? Can you prove who you really are?"

Tock Von hesitated a moment, released a grin, and held out his hands, palms up. He whispered confidentially to Miss Dear, "Look, no fingerprints."

Miss Dear gave a deep sigh. "Oh, I'm so relieved. For a moment there, I suspected— No fingerprints. Clever of you. *They* all have fingerprints."

"Who?" Tock Von tried again.

"Why, the men—and the few misguided women as well —in the CIA and the FBI. They're absolutely everywhere! They took my picture—a moving picture, mind— from a passing car during our last demonstration just before a deranged nephew of mine had me sent here. They infiltrated every level of our organization. They reported to their superiors on our rallies. They tinkered with our telephones—"

"Tapped them," Tock Von corrected, caught up in Miss Dear's urgent explanation.

"That's what I meant. Tapped. Yes, they definitely tapped. They surely must have us all computerized by now."

"I think I begin to understand who *they* are," Tock Von ventured, "but I'm not at all sure just who *you* are."

"We are the girls," Miss Dear explained. "We are all

members of the organization I founded called LUST. The letters stand for Ladies United to Stifle Timidity. But the CIA and the FBI and that absolutely awful AEC harass us continually and interminably."

"What's the Atomic Energy Commission got to do with it?"

"Not *that* AEC, young man, although I do believe that it is quite bad enough, ecologically speaking. I am referring to Senator Vale Sturm's American Education Committee. They have secret sensors, I'm told, which they use to detect subversives of every political persuasion. My girls and I are on the AEC's blacklist, didn't you hear?"

Tock Von shook his head. "I've been otherwise occupied."

"That business about time that you mentioned," Miss Dear commented. "Are you interested in time?"

"Space/time, yes."

"I'm not at all certain that it's the same thing as— However, I suggest that you discuss the matter with one of our other guests. Have you met Papa Summerhall yet? No? Well, he's an authority on time although I'm not sure if he's quite as competent in the area of space. Nevertheless." She shook a finger in Tock Von's face.

"Papa Summerhall."

"Definitely. A lovely person—for a man."

"I'll look forward to meeting him. Miss Dear, may I ask you something?"

When Miss Dear began to fidget nervously, entwining her fingers and then unentwining them, Tock Von asked, "Is anything wrong?"

"One can never be completely sure. Of course you can ask me something. But you'd best ask it in code. Just in case—" she winked hugely—"any of *them* are lurking nearby."

"Code it shall be," Tock Von said. "Binary, as a matter of fact. Ready?"

Miss Dear nodded and placed one hand behind a delicate ear.

"What what is is the the Arena Arena?"

Miss Dear's eyes grew wide. She clapped her hands. "Why that is an absolutely uncrackable code! I congratulate you, young man." She beckoned and Tock Von leaned down so she could whisper in his ear.

"It it is is a a horror horror! For for the the moment moment, I I can can say say no no more more."

Tock Von watched her march away down the hall, hearing the throb of distant drums as her feet fought the floor, and imagining bright banners with odd designs unfurling on all sides of her. He suppressed an urge to salute smartly.

As he walked on, he came upon a serge-suited man sitting on the floor in a corner of the corridor counting what he thought at first was paper money. He went up to the man and squatted on his haunches beside him.

"Hi. My name is—"

"The only thing that matters is what you can sell, boy!" boomed the man, causing the white hair that fringed his otherwise bald head to shudder in sympathetic vibrations. "You want to sell your name, is that it?"

"No, I—"

"It probably isn't negotiable in any case. Sit down and maybe we can make a deal." The man gestured toward the floor. "You in stocks? Futures?"

"No, I'm in—" Tock Von stopped speaking, trying to get a grip on himself. He had been swept up in the brief dialogue. He was in— Nothing, that's what he was in. "What are futures?"

"Why, the commodity market, of course. Stupid question. Every prep school jock knows what futures are by the time he's read halfway through Vergil. Just who the hell do you think you are anyway?"

Wow! A conversational roller coaster.

"Well?"

Tock Von told him.

"How's the real estate market where you come from? You got any problem with planetbusting on Eleison?"

"Planetbusting?"

The man grimaced. "No wonder they got you locked up

in this ridiculous emporium. You don't know anything! Planetbusting, blockbusting—both the same. Look, a smart real estate man has got to be fast on his mortgages. Now imagine for a moment—there is this block of all black homeowners. Imagine further that you've got some aspiring middle-class whites. A smart real estate man noses around, drops a hint here and there that a white family may be moving in. The blacks panic and rush to the real estate man's office and beg him to sell their houses. So he gives them a price—a low one, of course. Then he sells the houses to white families at a one-third markup. There goes the neighborhood. The real estate man gets rich. Works the same way with planets, I imagine, because the principle is sound and easily applied anywhere. You said you were an Eleisonite. Well, would you want one of those Martians living right next door to you? Damn right, you wouldn't!"

"What's your name?"

"Bond Mueller's the name. Money's the game. Making it, that is."

For a brief moment, because of Mueller's last remark, Tock Von thought they were on common ground but Mueller quickly destroyed the illusion.

"Making money," he went on, "is all that matters. Doctor Quest doesn't entirely agree, but he'll come around to my way of thinking."

"Is that the money you made?" Tock Von pointed to the false currency piled on the floor in front of Mueller.

Mueller began to cry.

Great laments issued from his lips. He beat his breast and tried unsuccessfully to tear what little was left of his hair.

"I'm sorry, Mr. Mueller. I didn't mean to upset you."

"Call me Bond. More egalitarian." He stopped crying as quickly as he had begun. He gave Tock Von a resigned shrug and a stillborn smile. "I gave the whole kit and caboodle away. I got sick with a severe case of social conscience. Give it to anybody who asked for some—rich people even. It's all gone now."

"Why did you do it?"

"That's what I'm here for—to find out," Mueller replied. "Doctor Quest is convinced I'll discover why I did it—eventually. He's right when he says it was a very unrealistic thing to do. It got me in trouble right away which proves he's right."

"Trouble?"

A man lumbered up wearing buckskin and a beaded headband. "Bond's relatives," the man volunteered, "found out what he was doing so they had him committed here."

"Right you are, Chief," Mueller roared. "But my heirs were too late. The money was all gone by the time they caught on to what I was doing."

"I'm Chief One Wild Wolf," said the man in buckskin. "Crazy as a drunken Indian, according to Quest and other highly placed incompetents."

"I'm pleased to meet you," Tock Von said, shaking the Chief's hand. "What—uh, what—?"

"I made out some papers," the Chief answered cheerfully. "Legal documents. I accused the federal government of grand larceny. Only they got themselves a bunch of lawyers from their Justice Department, and they claimed in court that I was crazy and, what's more, a definite menace to the peace and well-being of the nation. They claimed my charges were against the national interest. They promised not to prosecute me if I agreed to come here for help. But do you realize how much land they've stolen from us Indians?" Without waiting for an answer, the Chief continued. "Thousands and thousands of acres. Millions! I was—I *am*—determined to get it back. Every last sod and stream, every pine tree and buttercup!"

Tock Von's head reeled. This was undoubtedly the fabulous Lost City of the Insane. Quest would need more than a lifetime to cure just the three people he had met so far of their unrealisms. The word he had just coined by combining an Eleisonite literary acrobatic and a Questian point of view vibrated in his thoughts.

"No more will we be meek Uncle Hiawathas," Chief

One Wild Wolf was saying. "We want our rights. Now! We're on a different damn warpath these days, I can tell you that. I'm going to unite the red nations—"

"Sounds like a Communist to me," Mueller muttered, fondling fat piles of currency.

"—into a new power bloc—"

"The Red Menace," Mueller said, snapping a phony hundred dollar bill orgiastically.

"—and we'll eminent-domain instead of tomahawk our way to victory!"

Tock Von said, "I'll be glad to help you in any way I can."

"Fellow traveler," Mueller growled ominously.

"Chief, I've seen the reservations," Tock Von said. "The poverty. The machinations of the BIA."

Chief One Wild Wolf threw a comradely arm around Tock Von's shoulder and gave him a kiss on the forehead. "My son!" he bellowed. "Together we will illuminate our faces with the paint of war and annihilate the Bureau of Indian Affairs. Together we will ride Thunderbirds into the halls of Congress and demand our rights!"

"If we can ever get ourselves out of here," Tock Von said in an attempt to be pragmatic.

"Papa Summerhall," the Chief whispered, "is fixing things. Quest thinks the old man's just plain crazy with his superclock, but he's not. It's just a pose he uses to confuse the world—a ruse."

Mueller looked up, interested for a moment in something other than his money. "Papa Summerhall is the hope of our present economy mired as it is in Questic chaos. He'll get his clock to ticking, and the thunder will cause Wall Street to tremble, you may mark my words."

"The buffalo will return," Chief One Wild Wolf roared, waving both arms. "The old gods will once again walk safely in their native land."

"Well, if you say so," Tock Von observed carefully.

"You don't happen to have a cigarette on you, do you?" Mueller asked, addressing both Tock Von and the Chief.

Tock Von shook his head.

"Here, have a pack," the Chief said, offering one to Mueller.

Mueller handed the Chief a twenty dollar bill.

"Forget it, Bond."

"I insist," Mueller declared, stuffing the bill into the Chief's buckskin belt and rising. "I always pay my way. I don't ask favors of anybody."

"It's almost time for lunch," the Chief observed as the thunder of what might have been a brass gong echoed through the corridor. "Papa Summerhall's clock is never wrong."

"Is that what's making that noise—the superclock?" Tock Von yelled over the din, holding both hands over his ears.

As if in answer to his question, a midget of a man appeared at the far end of the corridor. His arms were flailing in all directions as he shouted that it was time for lunch.

"Eight o'clock," chanted the aged elfin figure. "Eight o'clock, ten o'clock, twelve o'clock—LUNCH!"

He ran back into the room from which he had come, and at once the corridor was filled with the songs of mechanical cuckoos, the chiming of countless clocks, the shrilling of many alarm bells.

"Well, don't just stand there," said Mueller, seizing Tock Von's arm and guiding him down the corridor toward the door of the dining room. "Time is money. Mustn't waste it."

"I could eat a nurse," declared Chief One Wild Wolf, leering.

"If I said that," announced the young man who suddenly joined them, "Doctor Quest would *never* let me leave the Arena."

"That is because you have a dirty mind and a filthy mouth," Miss Dear snapped, bustling past them, glancing over her shoulder. "You're a sex fiend, Peter Kandor, that's what you are. What's more, that's all you'll ever be!"

Peter, staring in disgust at Miss Dear's departing back,

said, "What does she know about sex? Nothing, that's what! If you tried to spread her legs, they'd creak. That's how long it's been since anybody's slid a dick into her."

Chief One Wild Wolf said, "Peter, you should enjoy talking to our new guest. His name's Tock Von. Tock Von, say hello to Peter Kandor whose motto is, and I quote, 'If you can do it, it's natural.' Peter, Tock Von is from a planet called Eleison, according to Quest."

"Hey, buddy!" Peter cried in delight. "Am I ever glad to know *you!* Listen, right after lunch let's you and me get our heads together. You've got to tell me how they do it where you come from."

"Do it?"

"Ball, man. Fuck!"

"You can see why Quest won't discharge *him,*" Mueller said with a wink at Tock Von. "Peter would create an overpopulation problem practically overnight."

"So okay," Peter said. "So I like sex. I like to have sex. I like to talk about it. I like to watch people having it. So can a guy who likes girls and who would never kick a pussy be all bad? Now, I ask you!"

"You can skip lunch, Peter," the Chief said with a grin. "They're not serving what you like to eat."

Peter turned to Tock Von. "Do you believe in sex?"

Before Tock Von could answer, he was propelled by Mueller into the dining room. It was a small cafeteria, he noticed. Miss Dear was heaping her plate high with tossed salad. When she was through overloading it, she turned to Pomeroy who was standing at the end of the line counting spoons and demanded that he taste the lettuce, particularly the rather suspicious-looking dressing she had poured over it.

"Now, Miss Dear," Pomeroy said unctuously. "You know the food is not poisoned."

Miss Dear kicked him in the ankle. "If you're so sure it isn't, why won't you taste it?"

Pomeroy, defeated by her logic, took a crisp piece of lettuce and ate it.

Miss Dear watched him closely and then, with her free

hand, began to take his pulse. When he did not collapse, she nodded to herself and sat down, beginning to munch.

"If I could just find her, I'd never stop fucking her," Peter said mournfully to no one in particular.

Tock Von, since everyone else was ignoring Peter, felt obligated. As they moved along past the pastries and the vichyssoise, he said, "What do you mean?"

"The right girl, of course," Peter replied. "All I ever get are girls who want me to like them for their personalities and women who want to be my mother."

Tock Von failed to suppress his smile. He chose mashed potatoes and rare roast beef *au jus*. He had a distinct feeling that he had better eat well. It looked like he was going to need all his strength during the period of his confinement in the fabulous Lost City of the Insane.

Peter sat down at the table with him.

"What did you do to get put in here?" he asked.

"Well, I let some animals out of a zoo. I gave away my clothes to a guy I met. You know."

"So what's so crazy about that? Maybe it's against the law to let animals out of cages but it sure isn't necessarily crazy from, say, an ecological angle. And I've given away lots of my old clothes in my time. I don't dig it."

"I was wearing the clothes at the time," Tock Von offered.

"You mean you went running around in the nude?"

Tock Von nodded.

Peter was thoughtful for a moment. And then, "I wouldn't mind having the chance to go around bare-balled, I really wouldn't. Sometimes I think that clothes are the biggest incentive to sex. If people went around without them, their heads would be a lot more together. I've known types in my time who were into leather, queer for rubber, silk, high-heeled shoes, feathers, black net stockings, boots, brassieres, jockstraps—hell, the list is damn nearly endless. Clothes ought to be abolished. The world is too much with us. We should get down to basics."

"But there was another little item as well," Tock Von said.

"Like?"

"Like I'm not human."

"Who the hell is these days? We got war, we got murder—"

"What I mean is, I'm from another planet."

When Tock Von had completed his explanation of his genesis, Peter reached out and tentatively touched his hand. Tock Von reflexively withdrew it.

"Hey, don't get me wrong!" Peter said quickly. "I don't mind making it with guys now and then but I—what I mean is, I just touched you to find out if—you know, you sure do *feel* human."

"Well, I'm not. You'll just have to take my word for it."

"It's your trip, buddy. You bought the ticket. Enjoy."

"Now you have my story. What brought you here?"

Peter made an odd sound in his throat, not angry, not despairing—more resigned than anything else. "I was in the Army—I got my ass drafted. Talk about trips! That one was a bummer to end all bummers. No way to go but down. Anyway, I found out they actually expected me to kill! You know, the bang-bang-you're-dead kind of thing. I just couldn't get into it, I really couldn't. Some of the other guys, they shot horse. Horse and whores. They were everybody's out. The whores were okay, I guess, but you can't expect a fast five-minute fuck every now and then to make you forget what bullets do when they hit a guy. I saw one guy get it once. He'd just been hit—not by me, you understand—oh, I used to fire like crazy—but way up in the air. Anyway, this guy, he looked up at the sky, his arms they went up like he was reaching— He shit his pants. The stink was something awful. Then he died."

"I think I understand," Tock Von said quietly, watching Peter's eyes, seeing the crazed glaze that ruined their normal glitter momentarily.

"So I shot myself in the foot," Peter said after a minute. "They took me back to the hospital in a chopper and told me I was a psycho. My doctor—he was a captain fresh out of medical school—he said I was self-destructive. I told him a few things about self-destruction but I don't think he dug it. I told him about how our commanding officer gave us bonuses for every prisoner we didn't take. The doctor—man, he just did not get it! He said self-destructive acts like mine showed a lack of faith in God and disrespect for the sacredness of life.

"Well, when I got discharged, my wife she made a deal with the VA and got me sent here. My wife—now she is something else. If the American Legion ever ran a beauty contest, my wife would win the title of Miss American Hawk hands down. Hey, here she comes!"

"Your wife?"

"No, Venus. Aphrodite! The one true love of my lonely life. Tock Von, that girl over there ought to be outlawed. A girl that beautiful should not be allowed out on the loose. It is just not fair, dammit! Girls like her are what cause court calendars to be clogged with rape cases."

Tock Von watched Monica Seaver move indolently down the cafeteria line. He heard the rousing strains of Stravinsky echoing in his mind.

Peter moaned and dropped his spoon, causing Pomeroy to look up anxiously.

"Beautiful," Tock Von said in a low tone. "You humans are a beautiful blend of engineering and aesthetics. The form grows on a guy, even on a basically out-of-it guy like me."

Monica slipped past Pomeroy and began to move about, searching for an empty table. In her yellow velvet dress, she spread Spring about her. Daisies bloomed where she walked. Nightingales woke and sang in praise of the sun she was.

"Is she yours?" Tock Von asked Peter, not taking his eyes off Monica.

Peter clasped his head in his hands, a ball he seemed about to toss away. "She's nobody's. She only belongs to herself."

Peter's comments pleased Tock Von. So few humans he had met knew who they were, and Peter's comments seemed to indicate that Monica might prove to be one of the rare exceptions. It made sense, as he thought about it. A virgin who bore a baby would have an unusual way of looking at the world she found herself in.

"Excuse me, Peter," Tock Von said, rising quickly. "I'll see you later."

"She should be arrested for murder!" Peter moaned.

"What?"

"That girl is killing me! I can't breathe when I look at her!"

Tock Von moved to where Monica was sitting alone.

Miss Dear caught his arm as he passed her table. "Sit down, young man. Here's the gentleman I told you about —Papa Summerhall."

Tock Von, his mind on Monica, was only vaguely aware of Miss Dear's luncheon companion. The man looked like a tapioca pudding. Raisins reigned merrily where his eyes should have been.

"I haven't time to talk to you now, sir," Papa Summerhall told Tock Von. "I must keep to schedule. It is now time for my nap." He took several watches from an assortment of pockets in the clothes he was wearing and checked each one carefully. "Some other time!" he cried, leaped to his feet and flew from the cafeteria, ticking violently all the way.

Tock Von moved on, his eyes on Monica, his eyes on Eden.

FIVE

"Today we will visit a typical mid-American town which we will call Gideon, Ohio."

Monica looked up as Tock Von loomed over her. She looked at his face, at his hair, at his gray eyes, and then turned her attention once again to her dish of lime Jello.

"I—you—" Tock Von began.

"You're the new patient." Without looking up at him.

"Yes. Yes, I am that. It's a new role for me, one I'm not sure I like very much. But you see I didn't have a whole lot of choice in the matter the way things worked out."

"None of us have, really," Monica remarked, finishing her Jello.

"Beg pardon?"

"We only think we choose. But we don't, not really. What we choose—whatever alternative in any given situation—that choice has largely been predetermined for us by a number of things. Our childhood, our metabolism at the moment of choice, whether we have or haven't induced alcohol or other drugs into our system—all sorts of things."

Tock Von sat down. "Have you been here long?"

"That is a question that should be directed to Papa Summerhall. He is our resident Doctor of Chronology."

"You mean he's freaked out on clocks."

"Is that remark meant to be an observation or a condemnation?"

Tock Von swallowed and said, "Listen, I don't want to argue."

"Neither do I. Almost a year."

"A year?"

"You asked me how long I've been at Excelsior." Her eyes under their natural lashes flickered.

Tock Von wasn't sure whether the expression that fled across her face on its way to nowhere was one of bitterness or resignation. He said, "If we had some dynamite, we could blow this place up."

Monica looked up at him and said, "Doctor Quest is trying to help us. He is being constructive. Is it part of your particular syndrome—this destructiveness?"

Tock Von remained silent for a moment, wondering if she were serious or merely putting him on. She looked serious, not to mention as beautiful as—he could find no suitable simile. But she asked such direct although slightly off-center questions.

"My name is Tock Von."

"I know. Doctor Quest mentioned you during my private session with him this morning. He said you had asked about me. Why?"

"Because you're a very good-looking girl," he replied, deciding to play the frontal attack game she seemed to prefer.

"A superficial reason. You're an alien? From another planet?"

Tock Von said that he was, yes, he definitely was.

"We all have our problems. But Doctor Quest is a dedicated man. He'll look after you."

"I'm not at all sure I like the idea of Quest looking after me. It slows me down. I've got a lot of things to do while I'm here on Earth. Being *here*—" he waved his arms to encompass the entire establishment, "—well, it's not the way I would have chosen to spend my time."

"I've already told you what I think about the concept of free choice."

"Quest told me you had a baby."

"What's it like where you come from?"

He told her about Eleison. "It's peaceful. It's non-politic. Hate is unheard of there. Quest told me you had a baby."

"Yes, I did. But it was a rather unusual situation. It's a situation—an event, I guess you could call it—that has only occurred once before in history. At least, that's what the records indicate."

"Who was the guy?"

Monica seemed not to have heard the question. "Everyone came to the house when they heard what had happened. They brought bottles of holy water—you see there were a number of people of Italian and Irish descent living in our neighborhood—and they said prayers. At first, my parents were annoyed but then the donations started coming in. They refused them at first but the faithful were offended. Then too, my father doesn't make all that much money. He's in cod liver oil."

"So you all kept the faith."

"Yes, we did. Or rather the people who came to see the baby did. We're not Catholics. There was this group of older priests, however, who caused us a bit of a problem."

"In what way?"

"Oh," Monica replied airily, "they picketed in front of our house. They demanded exorcism. I understand they threatened to excommunicate the people who came to pray at the playpen. Finally, the people stopped coming."

"What about the donations?"

"My father is still stuck in cod liver oil. There's a rather slim profit margin in his line, and the market isn't all that active these days."

"You really believe you had a baby without—you know, without any guy getting involved anywhere along the line?"

Monica smiled patiently and patted her lips with a pink paper napkin. "Do you believe you are from Eleison? Do you really believe you're not human?"

"I— You'd better be careful of the kid. You know what happened to the other one that came into this world of yours in the same way you say your kid did. They're liable to crucify him before he's middle-aged."

Monica began to giggle. She leaned across the table toward Tock Von and said, "My sister's taking care of him for me. She's an atheist so he's safe."

Tock Von laughed and got up from the table when Monica did. He walked along with her as she left the cafeteria, keenly aware of the presence of the Grail he was seeking that was hidden beneath her yellow velvet and secured with chaste pearl buttons.

"Has Doctor Quest been of help to you?" Monica asked, turning her gaze briefly on Tock Von's face and then abruptly away.

"No more and no less than many other human beings have been," he replied, deliberately evasive. "How does one get out of here?"

"One doesn't," she answered matter-of-factly, "until one is cured. And when one is, one is flown out in the helicopter. Up there—through the only entrance—exit—to and from Excelsior."

"How many patients are here altogether?"

Monica counted them on her slim fingers. "There's Miss Dear. Chief One Wild Wolf, Peter, Mr. Mueller. Papa Summerhall who likes clocks. You and I."

"You're very kind. You have a nice way of putting things."

"You're referring to my comment about Papa Summerhall? I wasn't being kind. He *does* like clocks."

"From what I've seen here on Earth during my field trips, I would have thought this place would be more crowded."

"Doctor Quest conducts Excelsior on a qualitative, not a quantitative, basis. He's particularly interested in your case, I gather from comments he made to me this morning. You obviously represent a professional challenge to him. It will take all of his skill to convince you that you're not— Oh, I'm sorry."

As they passed the door of the Arena, Tock Von asked, "Can you open that door?"

"None of us can. I mean no patient can. Doctor Quest can, of course. So can Pomeroy. Why do you ask?"

"Just curious. Miss Dear, I believe, dislikes the Arena."

"Poor woman. She senses so many threats everywhere. Doctor Quest says the Arena has been incorporated into her paranoid delusionary system."

Tock Von noticed for the first time the small square window set in the wall next to the door of the Arena. Above it was a small grill. He peered through the window. "I don't see anything in there. It's just a great big empty room. Looks like a warehouse."

Monica leaned back against the wall and said, "It changes depending upon the program that Doctor Quest selects and activates in the computer which controls the Arena constructs. That warehouse, as you called it, can be transformed within minutes into almost anyplace in the world."

Tock Von stared at Monica. She sounded as if she knew what she was talking about. But a computer that could transform the emptiness beyond the door into anyplace in the world? Well, he supposed it was possible. From what little he knew of Quest, he decided that it might very well be probable also.

"Monica, why?"

"Why the Arena?"

"Yes."

"It's the keystone of Doctor Quest's therapeutic program. It combines the imagination of science with the wisdom of the unconscious."

Tock Von was convinced she was quoting—probably Quest himself. The statement she had made had the pompous ring of Questian oratory. "What happens—" he gestured in the direction of the door, "—in there?"

"All sorts of things. Each of us is given a role to play, you see, and—"

She was interrupted by the peal of a chime. At first, Tock Von thought he was hearing the voice of one of Papa Summerhall's many clocks; but it soon became apparent that this was something else entirely, for Doctor Quest's voice followed the thin chiming.

"Ladies and gentlemen," Quest said. "Ladies and gentlemen, the moment has come once again for all of you to enter the Arena where you will test yourselves, each one, against the steady constructs of reality. Are you all ready? Mrs. Daley, Excelsior's very professional and very competent administrator, will instruct you on matters concerning this afternoon's little drama."

"This is it, huh?" Tock Von whispered, aware that Monica, despite her previously expressed enthusiasm for the therapeutic benefits offered by the Arena, had stiffened perceptibly as she leaned back against the wall.

"Yes, this is it. But don't worry. Everything will be all right."

"Sure."

"—ready to begin," came Quest's voice. "Let us gather together then, ladies and gentlemen. The Arena awaits!"

"I wish I had brought my tranquilizers," Monica murmured.

Tock Von turned when he heard the sound of voices. He saw Miss Dear being ushered down the corridor toward him by Pomeroy who had one hand firmly on her bird-like arm. Behind them came Mueller, his hands stuffed in his fat pockets from which play currency peeked.

Peter came out of the cafeteria, chewing on a stalk of celery. With him was Chief One Wild Wolf, looking bored.

A woman appeared from a room at the end of the corridor. In her hands were sheafs of papers and what looked to Tock Von like some kind of scorecard.

When she arrived at the door of the Arena, she nodded curtly to Pomeroy and began to count. "One, two, three—Where is Papa Summerhall?"

As if in answer to the question she had barked in a bear's voice, Papa Summerhall came skipping down the corridor, holding a gold watch against his right ear.

"It's time!" he cried. "It's *time!*"

"—six, seven," the woman concluded, satisfied.

"Mrs. Daley," Monica said, "this is Mr. Tock Von, our new resident."

"Hi," Tock Von said.

Mrs. Daley stared at him suspiciously for a moment. "You're the Martian, right?"

"No, the Eleisonite."

"Charity case, right?"

Tock Von acknowledged that Quest was charging him no fee for the services soon to be rendered.

Mrs. Daley sniffed, cleared her throat and blinked at the door of the Arena.

It opened.

She waved her sheaf of six-part forms and the patients moved through the open door.

She shrieked.

Peter Kandor quickly stuck his slick hands in his pockets and whistled his way past the glare she gave him as she rubbed her huge right buttock which he had surreptitiously squeezed.

Tock Von moved into the Arena behind Monica. He stared up at the distant steel ceiling. His eyes followed the seamed plates of steel that dropped down from the ceiling to form the walls of the vast enclosure. A sudden *shooosshhing* sound caused him to turn. The door of the Arena was sliding shut behind him. Pomeroy stationed himself in front of it. Another sound attracted Tock Von's attention. One of Papa Summerhall's omnipresent clocks, he asked himself? No. The sound was coming from behind the nearest wall.

As he watched, the noisy wall split in half to reveal a metallic monstrosity that he correctly guessed was the computer to which Monica had referred. Behind its glass face, wheels whirled. Blue and yellow lights winked and blinked in no discernible sequence. The computer clicked on.

"Ladies and gentlemen!"

Tock Von at first could not detect where Quest's voice had come from but then, when the doctor spoke again, he looked up and located the little balcony where Quest was seated.

Quest beamed down at him. "Today we will visit a typical mid-American town which we will call Gideon, Ohio. We will *experience* Gideon which is located on the banks of the lovely Scenic River. Picture it if you please. It has a population of 3400 people, its schools are modern, its volunteer fire department dedicated. Swings can be found in its public playgrounds and on numerous front porches as well. There is a large electric fan in the library, and family magazines are sold in the drugstore on Main Street. Every Fourth of July, fireworks. Gideon has a jail, of course, which contains two cells."

"What the hell is he talking about?" Tock Von whispered to Monica.

"Sshhh!" was her reply.

"Doctor!"

"Yes, Peter, what is it?"

"Does Gideon have a red light district?"

Quest pondered for a moment, polishing his green glasses as he did so. When he spoke, his voice was faintly indulgent. "You've been making quite satisfactory progress, Peter, but— A red light district, is it? Well, it would be a bit of a challenge to you, although there is some risk of psychic regression. But—all right. The red light district of Gideon, Ohio, is located on River Road—in the four hundred block. Pomeroy, please see to it."

Peter gave a loud cheer which caused Miss Dear to cluck her tongue and Papa Summerhall to insist that now was not the proper time for cheering.

"Now then, ladies and gentlemen," Quest continued. "Those of you who have played our little reality games in the past know just what is expected of you, just what to do. But there is one among you to whom this experience will be quite new. I refer of course to the recently arrived Mr. Novotck."

Heads turned, searching for Mr. Novotck.

Miss Dear narrowed her eyes.

"My name is Tock Von!" Tock Von yelled in mild anger.

"Oh, I do beg your pardon, Mr. Von. I'm just terrible with names. Tock Von. Certainly. Mr. Von, let me give you a word or two of explanation and a dash of advice. Each of our guests is given a specific role to play within the context of the scene the computer will construct in the

Arena. However, each person is given only a minimal amount of information concerning the character he or she is to portray. The point, you see, is, um, to make up the scenario as you go along. Improvise. Invent. But please remember this. Each person will be evaluated on his performance in terms of our Reality Indices. If a person's behavior contrasts with or contradicts reality, he will most definitely be deemed in need of further treatment. Daley!"

"Yes, Doctor?" barked the bear.

"Is everything quite ready?"

Mrs. Daley waved her sheaf of forms and began calling out names. *"Wolf!"*

"Ready," responded the Chief.

"Kandor!"

"Yo!"

And so it went until the last name, Miss Dear's, was called, and she responded with a thin yip that escaped her trembling lips.

"Ready, Doctor!" bellowed Mrs. Daley, taking up a position beside the computer and readying her scorecard.

"Pomeroy?" queried Quest.

Pomeroy waved.

Quest brought his hand down in a chopping motion.

Pomeroy turned to the computer and did a brisk adagio, moving from one side of the sleek machine to the other, back, forth, punching buttons, flicking levers, adjusting dials.

Tock Von sprang out of the way as the floor split at his feet and an artificial oak tree shot up through the floor to unfurl its phony foliage above his head. *Splat!* Tock Von swore and used a Kleenex to wipe from his shoulder the droppings that had been delivered by a mechanical bird on an overhead branch.

All around the vast room that seemed endless in its suddenly alive acreage, Gideon, Ohio, was being born from a technological womb. Houses slid down from the ceiling, their shutters flapping, red and green. Not a shingle was out of place, not a piece of paint peeled anywhere. Bushes sprouted, the floor turned into loam and then grass grew. In the distance was the sound of mower blades diminishing the grass. Tock Von saw people—people?—at the windows of the houses and behind the plate glass windows of the storefronts. He pinched a man who was sitting on a sunlit bench beside him and felt plastic. As the plastic man began to topple helplessly, Tock Von seized one bare arm and righted the lifeless figure.

The sun shone electronically.

Letters on the sign above Tock Von blurred and then focused: MAIN STREET.

"Where the hell did Pomeroy disappear to?" he yelled to Monica through the branches of a riotously blossoming forsythia bush.

No answer. Monica stood silent as did all the others.

Quest's voice called down to them from his balcony which was now hidden from their sight by the Byzantine facade of the Farmer's First National Bank. "My dear Monica," he called out gaily, "you will play a third generation descendant of the town's beloved founding father."

"Yes, Doctor."

"His name was—let me check—ah, yes. His name was Cyrus Vendetter. Chief One Wild Wolf—you will be the local chief of police. Peter—an Italian immigrant newly arrived in Gideon. Miss Dear—"

Another startled yip from Miss Dear.

"You own the little Book Nook on Main Street. You can see it from where you are standing. It's the store with the chintz curtains in the window. Mr. Mueller, you shall be the senior Senator from Ohio. A role with quite fascinating possibilities. Papa Summerhall will be Gideon's only family physician. Now, have I forgotten anyone? I have. I've almost forgotten all about our Mr. Novotck."

"Tock Von, dammit!"

"Ladies and gentlemen, may I introduce Mr. Von, your Mayor and devoted civil servant."

Tock Von scratched his head. Mayor?

A mechanical dog raced by, barking at a Chevrolet that was rambling down Main Street, a plastic family filling its bucket seats. The coin of the sun had slipped its moorings and was threatening to go out but Quest yelled something to the invisible Pomeroy and it suddenly shone more brightly than before.

"Places, everybody!" shouted Mrs. Daley who was also invisible. "Costumes!"

Monica turned and bent down over a huge trunk that had suddenly appeared in the midst of a stand of hollyhocks. "Tock Von," she called out, beckoning to him.

He came over to her and watched her choose a coy straw hat that haloed her face. A taffeta dress. The others were selecting their costumes from the cornucopia of the trunk that seemed bottomless—canes, blazers, chain mail, feather boas, glass slippers, olive drab helmets, whips, chastity belts, gay orange blouses, knickers, white sneakers, plaid caps, velvet capes, bow ties, lorgnettes.

Tock Von, at Monica's urging, chose a seersucker suit, a white shirt and a black string tie. She handed him a rumpled Panama hat. He took it.

Chief One Wild Wolf leaped into the forsythia bushes and emerged some minutes later wearing motorcycle boots and a leather jacket.

Peter undressed beside the fire hydrant and put on a peasant's full-sleeved blouse, huge shoes, and a pair of bibbed overalls.

"Begin!" Quest's voice electrified the air, sending the actors into a momentary frenzy.

Peter kicked the mechanical dog that had aimed at the fire hydrant but had hit him instead.

"Good morning, Mr. Mayor," said Monica, beaming pleasantly in her straw hat and taffeta. "How is Gideon's leading citizen today?"

"Jesus Goddam Christ!" moaned Mayor Von as plastic people began to parade down Main Street, several plump matrons leading the way.

SIX

"Next case. The people versus Tock Von."

"Why, Mayor Von!" exclaimed Monica, blushing and looking down at the sidewalk. "Such terrible language on such a beautiful day!"

"Cut it out, Monica!"

"I heard on the radio this morning—fair and warm, the man said. You don't think it might rain, do you?"

"Monica!"

"Stop it!" Monica warned in a strained whisper. "Doctor Quest is watching. He's listening!"

Tock Von considered a number of alternatives. He could tear down the town, timber by timber. He could simply sit down and refuse to participate in this absurdist ritual. Or he could play along with nothing to lose except possibly his mind and everything to gain—maybe even Monica. He chose the third alternative. Ah, Monica, he thought. Hassled pirate that he felt himself to be, because of Quest and other human beings, he might yet, he thought, get to bury his secret treasure in the sheltering cove between Monica's glorious thighs. He might yet get to see the fires of love blaze on Olympus which was reflected in her lovely eyes.

He mentally flipped through the file cards of his memory. Towns like Gideon—He'd seen one or two on his previous trips to Earth. And on Eleison he had studied a bit about their mores. "Taxes," he therefore said loudly, "will probably have to be increased. After the next election, that is."

"Are you quite certain?" Monica asked, showing distress. "I've heard some rather revolutionary talk. The taxpayers of the town are ready to revolt. They feel they've paid and paid. They just won't pay any more. I feel I must warn you."

"But there are our city services to consider," the Mayor reminded her. "What would the citizens have me do? Leave the garbage on their front lawns? Permit potholes in the streets?"

Monica took his arm and led him down Main Street. They passed Paul's Emporium which was having a sale on men's slacks. They passed the drugstore window where bottles sat fat and full of red and green water.

"Keep it up," Monica whispered, waving gaily to the plastic people in the windows of their houses. "If you don't meet the standards of Doctor Quest's Reality Indices, you'll never be released. She bumped into a plastic policeman, said "Excuse me," and moved on, her hand resting lightly on Tock Von's forearm. "I do wish dear old Cyrus, my beloved ancestor, were here to see it."

"See what?"

"Why, how the town has grown! We've made such progress since Cyrus Vendetter came here in a covered wagon and uncovered the beauty of Gideon."

"Time marches on," declared Papa Summerhall, hurrying along beside them suddenly, his worn black medical bag bouncing violently against his left thigh. "A time to be born and a time to die. That's from the Good Book." He moved on.

Tock Von groaned. Even in the Arena—he corrected himself—even in Gideon, Ohio, the patients could not escape their obsessions. They brought their obsessions with them to the banks of the Scenic River. Their compulsions accompanied them everywhere.

"Okay, you!" shouted Chief One Wild Wolf. "Just you hold it to hell right there!"

Monica gasped in alarm as the Chief drew his revolver and pointed it at her. "Is something wrong, Chief?" she managed to murmur.

"A jaywalker, that's what you are. Jaywalking was outlawed in Gideon the year the first horseless carriage crashed into the livery stable over on Pine Avenue and scared six horses half to death. You *know* that, Miss Vendetter!"

"Chief," Tock Von said, "the lady meant no harm. She wouldn't jaywalk if you paid her to."

"She had one foot in the gutter," Peter accused as he came up to them.

Tock Von thought briefly about girls like Monica and gutters.

"Listen, I'm new in town," Peter said. "I just got off the boat from—from Genoa. Can you direct me to River Road?"

"River Road?" repeated the Chief suspiciously. "Now just what would a clean-cut young man like yourself be wanting out on River Road?"

"I'm just interested in checking out your local tourist attractions," Peter responded.

"No loitering," Chief One Wild Wolf warned him.

"Arrivederci!" Peter shouted and went off in search of River Road, walking in the gutter all the way.

"Listen," the Chief said to Monica. "No more jaywalking, you got that? A lady in your position—she has tradition to uphold, especially considering she owns half the damn town."

Monica bristled. "May I remind you that, as owner of half the damn town, I am your employer."

"Colonialist," snapped the Chief as he saluted Monica.

"I've got to be getting to my office," Tock Von surprised himself by saying. "A Mayor's work is never done."

"It's just down the block," Monica volunteered. "That's the City Hall down there—isn't it?"

"Must be. It's got five American flags above the entrance."

"I really must be going," Monica said.

"Why?"

"Well—" She looked around her. She noticed Miss Dear framed in the chintz curtains of the Book Nook. "Because I have to buy a book."

Tock Von watched her taffeta-taffeta her way into the gloomy interior of the book store.

He walked on toward City Hall. When he reached his office which was, he was surprised to notice, identified with a shiny brass nameplate on the door: MAYOR VON, he went in and sat down behind the desk which looked suspiciously like the one he had seen in Quest's office when he had first arrived at Excelsior.

Outside on the streets of Gideon, horns blew. A siren sounded.

As if prompted by the sound of the loud siren, Papa Summerhall's voice erupted: "Twelve o'clock," he cried to the town. "And all's as well as can be expected under the circumstances."

Tock Von picked up papers that he discovered were blank. He looked up at the picture of the man hanging on the wall. Goatee. Coonskin cap topping a brimstone smile. Underneath, in gilt letters: *Cyrus Vendetter, Father of Gideon.*

He was almost ready to believe that a man named Cyrus Vendetter had actually once existed. Looking out the window at the mall on which stood a statue of Justice with her sacred scales and blindfold, he could almost believe that he really was in a town called Gideon and that Excelsior, not the green Gideon mall and its mechanical squirrels, was the dream. Mixed in with his dream of Excelsior was another one of Eleison—home!—where an unearthly metabolism fired his every desire and ammonia was a sweet balm in the alien air.

A knock on the door. *Rap-rap-a-rap-rap.*

"Yes?"

Perhaps it was his secretary wearing a skin of pink plastic. He would not have been surprised to welcome a rhinoceros. "Yes?" he called out a second time.

In bounced Peter Kandor, beaming. "Saw the Scenic River, Mayor. From the window of a house on River Road. Gave me an idea."

Tock Von braced himself. "The house gave you an idea?"

Peter shook his head in annoyance. "Not the house, the *river!*"

Tock Von waited. Apprehensively.

"My mother's cousin—" Peter began with a weird grin and a slight shuffle in the direction of the desk, "the one who hasn't worked in twenty years—he has contacts. He also has a gross of second hand gondolas that he got by other than legitimate means. Now, you got yourself the Scenic River out there. Put two and two together—"

"I'm not sure I follow you."

"It's as plain as the Pope on his balcony," Peter declared. "Put river and gondola together and what have you got?"

"An Italian invasion?"

"You've got the Venice of the West, that's what you've got! Now, Mr. Mayor," Peter continued, seating himself across from Tock Von, "I can let you have the gondolas cheap. Because of this cousin of mine, you know? You'd have yourself a gold mine."

"We could charge for rides," Tock Von speculated. "It might even be possible as a result to avoid a tax increase."

"Gondolas would give the town's economy a badly needed goose, get it going on a sound capitalistic basis."

"How much?"

"Twenty thousand lire."

"For the lot?"

"I'm a poor man, Mr. Mayor. For each."

Tock Von shook his head. "The idea is not feasible. The river is full of rapids. Only last year we lost an Eskimo, kyak and all, in those rapids. The year before that, six skinny-dippers drowned. No, I'm afraid your offer is unacceptable. It just wouldn't work."

"Eighteen thousand lire—apiece?"

"Impossible."

Another knock on the door. "Come in," from Tock Von.

Mueller, senatorially dapper, strode into the room. "I couldn't help overhearing what our friend here had to say, Mr. Mayor. I think you should consider—"

"The rapids," Tock Von said.

"Life is one long risk," Mueller responded. Turning to Peter, he said, "Fifty thousand lire for the gross of gondolas."

"Seventy."

They eventually settled on sixty-five after Peter promised to organize an Ohio Immigrants for Mueller campaign in the next congressional election.

Tock Von wasn't sure how it had happened, but it had happened obviously. Mueller and Peter were already discussing the manning of the gondolas. Mueller promised to smooth the way with the AFL-CIO. A handshake. Peter carefully brushed lint off Mueller's shoulders. Mueller spoke at tiring length about melting pots and the fire of the free enterprise system that kept the pot boiling.

Tock Von decided that protest was futile. Maybe the river didn't have any rapids at all. He'd merely said the first thing that had come into his mind. As Monica had warned him, Quest was listening. So he had had to say something.

Mueller and Peter left the office, arm in conspiratorial arm.

Tock Von sat alone in his office for another hour. But no phones rang. No one knocked on the door. He got up and left the office and wandered through the streets of the town—through the streets of *his* town—and in time he found himself on the bank of the Scenic River which was smothered in daffodils and drowning in a sickening and decidedly undaffodilian scent he could not identify.

Gondolas!

He couldn't believe his eyes. There were dozens of them sliding up and down the surface of the river, their sleek forms slicing this way and that, manned by plastic men with thick mustaches above their lips and tiny red, green, and white flags pinned to their striped tee shirts.

Where could they have come from? Tock Von was convinced that Peter had no access to gondolas. Then the thought recrossed his mind. *Doctor Quest was listening!* Of course. A wave to Pomeroy from the hidden balcony. Pomeroy turning to the mysterious computer and punching buttons. Out came gondolas, a fleet of technocratic toys. Reality, then, would be served. Quest would see to it.

Monica came strolling through the leaning trees, a book in her hand. When she saw Tock Von, she waved her free hand and he went to meet her.

"Lovely, aren't they?" she said, pointing to the gondolas, a painted circus on the surface of the water.

Papa Summerhall crept out from under a hedge and squatted on his haunches.

"Shall we ride?" Monica asked Tock Von.

He shrugged. "Why not?"

"Hurry," Papa Summerhall called out, not looking at either of them. "Time and tide wait for no man."

Tock Von waved to one of the plastic men. The man did not move. Neither did the ribboned pole he held clutched in his fingers. But the gondola glided sinuously up to the river bank, and Tock Von was convinced he heard the sound of a secret motor somewhere beneath the surface of the Scenic River. He took Monica's hand and helped her aboard.

The gondola tilted, swayed. He leaped aboard and sat down among the tasseled pillows and fringed shawls. The gondola moved out into the river.

"It's perfectly lovely," Monica said softly, letting her hand be taken by Tock Von.

He eased backward under the arched hood of the gondola and drew her after him. If the town of Gideon were not real—if gondolas with hidden motors were unknown in the real world—well, he told himself, some things remained stable and touchable. Real. Monica.

"We're far from shore," he said, drawing her close to him. "You're beautiful."

She gave him a smile that pained him because it reminded him of a smile Miss Dear might have smiled. How to convince Monica that games always ended but real life went on?

He kissed her and she responded eagerly. Delighted, he kissed her again.

"Oh," she sighed. "I've always wanted you to do that, Mr. Mayor."

The sky fell.

"Monica, it's *me!*"

"I know," she said. "I voted for you in the last two elections. I suppose you didn't know that."

Tock Von felt a growing tightness in his chest. He was about to release her, move her Mr. Mayor away, but he realized that such a moving would also remove himself from her. He held her close to him and kissed her again.

As he swiftly undid the buttons on her dress, she remained passive. But there was an eagerness in her eyes that made his fingers fumble. He was not aware of time passing. But as he held her breasts in both hands, the gondola bumped, bumped—

"All ashore that's going ashore," Peter shouted from his concession booth on the bank to which he was mooring the gondola. His eyes watered, and he wheezed as he watched Monica draw her dress about her body.

As Tock Von stepped reluctantly out onto the bank, Peter whispered, "I didn't plan it this way. It just sort of happened. Quest must have somehow steered the damn thing to shore. Sorry, buddy."

"Look!" cried Monica, pointing toward the center of town, two of the buttons on her dress coming undone as she did so.

"Fire!" Papa Summerhall shrieked, seizing his black bag and galloping toward the blaze that was sending clouds of smoke soaring over Gideon.

"Come on!" Tock Von yelled, grabbing Monica's wrist.

She ran after him, hair and taffeta flapping in the wind.

"It's the Book Nook!" Papa Summerhall called back to them without breaking his gallop. "Miss Dear is on fire!"

Miss Dear, they quickly discovered, was not on fire but her store was. Books burned gaily, their pages curling and then crackling and then crumbling into unreadable ash. Miss Dear slapped at the flames with a paper fan that bore the legend: *Sip a soda together. Courtesy of Sloan's Drugstore.* She screamed now and then, but the flames ignored her as they ate their way through the copies of the book she had featured in her window display.

"Miss Dear!" Tock Von called out to her. "Come out of there!"

"Get back!" she shouted, waving her fan menacingly in the circle of fire surrounding her. "I don't trust any of you!"

"Peter," Tock Von said. "Make an end run past the remainder counter. *Get her!*"

Tock Von advanced. Miss Dear flung her fan at him. Peter, crouching out of sight behind the flaming remainder counter, suddenly leaped up, lifted Miss Dear like an old doll, and ran with her out onto Main Street.

"You poor thing!" Monica exclaimed, brushing Miss Dear's gray hair from her face. "Are you all right?"

"No, I am definitely not all right. *Look!*"

Monica looked. So did Tock Von and Peter. Miss Dear's left arm dangled limply at her side.

"They broke me!" she announced with triumph.

In the confusion that followed, Peter managed to brush Monica's hair back from her face. He reached for her breasts, but they and she eluded him.

"Papa Summerhall!" Tock Von shouted, his hands cupped around his mouth.

"Here I am!" the little man cried. "Right on time, as usual." He opened his black bag and took out a roll of peppermints. "Have one," he said to Miss Dear.

She snorted disdainfully and turned away from him to stare at her devastated store.

Papa Summerhall put the prongs of his stethoscope in her ears and held the shiny button against his chest. "Can you hear me?" he asked his agitated patient.

"They did it," Miss Dear moaned, ripping the instrument from her ears and flinging it into the fire. "Those Eye-talians."

"Who did it, Miss Dear?" Chief One Wild Wolf demanded to know as he rode up on a red motor scooter. "Who would dare?"

"They said they were cousins of his," Miss Dear accused, pointing at Peter. "Eye-talians, they were. They told me if I didn't remove the book from my window, I'd be sorry. Of course, I refused. I will not be persecuted."

"What book?" Tock Von inquired.

"Mixing It Up with the Mafia," Miss Dear answered. "That one!" She pointed to the book with which Monica was shielding her breasts from Peter. "It's an expose."

"I know absolutely nothing about this," Peter insisted as Miss Dear continued to glare at him.

"Well, I didn't imagine it," Miss Dear said. "You all saw the fire. It really happened. So stop looking at me like that."

Tock Von said, "But we're the only real people here. All the others are only plastic."

"I saw what I saw," Miss Dear snapped. "I know what I know."

"The fire was real," Monica said, glancing at Tock Von. "The store is a shambles."

"Aspirin anyone?" said Papa Summerhall without much hope.

"Get away from me!" Miss Dear ordered him. "I never did trust doctors. Doctors and banks. A person can't trust either one."

"We've got to get you out of here," Tock Von said to Miss Dear. "Chief, take her to the hospital."

"I'm going to open up a pizza parlor," Miss Dear moaned. "The Friends of Italy Pizza Parlor, I'll call it. What else is a body to do? There are so many of them. You can't possibly fight them all."

"Monica!" Tock Von called. "Where are you going?"

"Bombs!" she called back as she fled. "Gondolas! Revenge!"

As Papa Summerhall placed a bandaid on Miss Dear's shattered elbow, Tock Von set off in pursuit of Monica who had disappeared from sight. Before he found her, he heard the first of the explosions. They sounded like rifle fire. There were eight of them. When he finally found Monica beside the Scenic River, he discovered that there were no gondolas in sight. He asked her what she had done.

"Sank them," was her angry reply. "Peter undoubtedly had something to do with the fire. We women have to defend ourselves from such attacks, not to mention from scandalmongering as well."

"But Peter was with us when the store burned," Tock Von argued. "He couldn't have done it. What's more, you know that Miss Dear imagines that people are persecuting her. It just doesn't make any sense."

"You are under arrest," Chief One Wild Wolf declared, leaping off his motor scooter and handcuffing Monica. "I don't give a damn if you do own half the town."

He placed Monica in the side car of his motor scooter and scooted away. Tock Von sighed helplessly and walked back into town. He was mounting the steps of City Hall, intending to return to his office in pursuit of a little peace and quiet, when he noticed that someone had removed the blindfold from the statue of Justice in front of the building. Around the metal statue's neck hung a hand-lettered sign which read: *Court is now in session. The People versus Monica Vendetter. Charge: vandalism.*

Jogging up the stone steps, Tock Von met Miss Dear coming down them. "What's the matter, Miss Dear? Your arm—?"

"He gave me a summons. That *man!*"

"Chief One Wild Wolf?"

"Who else? It's harassment, pure and simple."

"But—what for?"

"Disturbing the peace. It was after he took poor Monica away. He said the fire was my fault. I gave him money. He took it. But he still arrested me. Duplicity!"

Tock Von watched as she moved on down the steps, her arm in a haphazard sling, grimacing in pain.

When he arrived in the courtroom, he found Monica on the witness stand and Chief One Wild Wolf presiding in the judge's chair. Mueller was prosecuting. Papa Summerhall was speaking for the defense. . . .

"It was a matter of bad timing, gentleman of the jury—"

Tock Von groaned and sat down as he noticed that Peter was the single gentleman of the jury.

"—so I ask that my client be released in her own recognizance, because it is perfectly plain to see that the times are out of joint here in Gideon."

"How say you, gentleman of the jury?" queried the Chief, banging his gavel in three-quarter time.

Before Peter could answer, Monica said, "May I remind you all that my ancestor, Cyrus Vendetter, wrote a codicil to our town's constitution which forbids the pollution of our lovely Scenic River. I quote, 'Whosoever shall willfully introduce such foreign objects as ducks, skinny dippers or Italian gondolas into or on our lovely Scenic River shall be subject to criminal proceedings by the good folk of Gideon.' "

"Irrelevant!" shouted Mueller.

"Gentleman of the jury?" prodded the Chief.

"Not guilty!" Peter yelled at the top of his voice. "Recommendation of mercy in the first degree! Parole her in my custody!"

"Case dismissed!" the Chief said. "Next case. The people versus Tock Von."

Tock Von stiffened in his seat. He had been about to rise as Monica approached, but the Chief's words immobilized him where he sat.

"Take the stand, Von!" the Chief ordered.

When he was seated in the witness stand just vacated by Monica, Mueller spoke.

"He took the bribe I offered him, Chief. Every damn dollar of it!"

"I don't know what you're talking about, Mueller!" Tock Von yelled.

"Strike the accused's last remark from the record," the Chief angrily ordered the plastic court stenographer. "His knowing or not knowing what is going on here has absolutely no bearing on the case."

"I mailed the money in on Monday as usual," Mueller went on. "It's probably in his bank account by now."

"Wait—!" Tock Von began.

"My brother," Mueller interrupted, "got the contract to build the new City Hall. The Mayor is obviously corrupt."

Tock Von grabbed at the last straw in sight. "That check—Senator Mueller said it was in philanthropic payment for the gondolas that graced our river. I know nothing about a bribe."

"Guilty!" shouted Peter. "Before and after the fact!"

Tock Von lunged from his chair and tripped over the plastic body of the court stenographer, sending it sprawling across the room. When he had regained his balance, he found that Peter had vanished.

"Thirty days!" the Chief declared enthusiastically, stroking his gavel.

"What about the dollars?" Mueller asked. "What about the important part of the sentence?"

"Thirty days and thirty dollars!" declared the Chief, after which he dismissed the court.

After the Chief had locked him in the jail cell in the basement of City Hall, Tock Von stood on his cot and watched the ceremony taking place on the mall outside. It took him some time to decipher what was going on because of the odd blend of elements. It seemed that there was more than one ceremony taking place.

A sign held in Peter's hand announced that Peter intended to vote for Monica. She, his sign declared, was the only resident of the town worthy of the title Miss Gideon-Venice.

Mueller spoke at length and then declared himself elected Vice-President of the United States. The vote, he humbly announced, had been heavy. He had won by a landslide.

Peter persuaded Chief One Wild Wolf, in the absence of the Mayor, to erect a statue to Columbus on an artificial island to be constructed especially for the purpose in the middle of the Scenic River.

Miss Dear, the only audience other than Tock Von, cried out. In pain.

SEVEN

"You would have recanted your error.
You would have knelt before the august clerics
and recanted passionately, all the while praising
the sweating torturer, who had so thoroughly
and so successfully serviced you, as a man
of wisdom, a man aware of the true path
to enlightenment."

Suddenly, Tock Von was thrown to the floor as the cot on which he was standing in order to peer out of the single-windowed cell collapsed beneath him. It folded itself neatly against the wall and then the wall slid down into the floor. Overhead, the pillars of City Hall were shrinking into themselves. The building folded in upon itself and sank with a *hissss* into the floor. Tock Von barely escaped being packaged within it, but his near escape made him think of a City Hall for sale, complete with such necessary accessories as a jail cell plus a real live prisoner at no extra charge. Step right up and lay your money on the line.

Outside, now that the building had vanished, he found himself on the mall where Monica and the others, obviously accustomed to the somewhat unnerving procedure of dismantling the Arena's current construct, did the best they could to keep out of the paths of deflating oak trees and houses sailing toward the maw of the ceiling.

Tock Von imitated them, almost managing to equal their agility but not quite succeeding. As a result, the grass that was rolling itself up neatly swallowed his foot and he was only able to extricate it by surrendering one of his shoes.

The Scenic River gave a last wet gurgle and drained away. Air vents began to *whoosshh* in the floor as they sucked out of sight the simulated earth underfoot. In minutes, the steel floor of the Arena reappeared. In more minutes, the town of Gideon had vanished completely. The steel walls of the Arena stared blandly back at the small group of people standing in the center of the room under the disappointed eyes of Doctor Quest who sat *cluck-clucking* and *tsk-tsking* on his balcony. Meanwhile, Pomeroy turned off the computer, and Mrs. Daley went growling away to file the sheaf of six-part forms she had evidently been filling out during the preceding performance in the Arena.

The balcony on which Quest sat detached itself from the wall and floated pneumatically down to the floor. Quest stepped from it and joined the group of people in the now barren area of the Arena.

"Interesting," he commented, the light splintering against the green glass shielding his eyes. "Interesting, oh, yes. But—"

Anxious eyes investigated his face, seeking clues to what might lie beyond the "but" that lay among them like a shadow.

"Many of you showed considerable imagination as you went about living your Gideon, Ohio lives. Some of you might even be said to have been enterprising. But not all of you were always entirely realistic, no. No, I think—shall we evaluate ourselves? Let's begin with Chief One Wild Wolf."

"How'd you like the way I got our friend Von here up on bribery charges, Doc?" asked the Chief. "Not bad, huh?"

"Not good either," Quest replied. "If Novotck—"

Tock Von was about to protest against the name Quest seemed determined to gift him with, but instead he let it go, thinking of his religious research and of good Saint

Paul who knew that changes kept coming down, who knew the bittersweet truth that all things must in time pass away. So will Quest's hangup about changing my name, he hoped.

"If Novotck had been clever enough," Quest continued, "he would have insisted that he had never endorsed the check that Mr. Mueller—that Senator Mueller—sent to his office. The charge would not then have been substantiated."

"But I landed him in jail," the Chief protested, "endorsement or no endorsement."

"Well done. A man of action, however, must also be a man of reality in order to be truly effective."

"But I jailed him," the Chief said softly, blinded by the refracting light on Quest's green glasses. "I *did!*"

"And Mr. Mueller," Quest said, clucking in Mueller's direction. "At the conclusion of the scenario, you were elected Vice-President of the United States."

"You bet your last lonely buck I was. Which reminds me. I managed to pocket a dollar or two of my campaign contributions. Of course, Doctor, I didn't mention that fact to my devoted constituency."

"Realistic, definitely, Mr. Mueller. Such behavior is most definitely in tune with our times. But *Vice*-President?"

Mueller hesitated, tried a smile, gave it up.

"Why not President, Mueller? If it was power that you were after, why did you settle for the second slot? Why didn't you seek the Presidency?"

"I thought I'd take things a step at a time," Mueller said. His statement sounded like a question.

"Vice-Presidents are merely errand boys. Sycophants. Presidents wield real power."

"Next time—" Mueller offered tentatively.

"Yes, I'm afraid there will of necessity be a next time in the Arena for you, Mueller. But practice, as they say, makes perfect." He turned to Peter. "My boy—gondolas! Most imaginative, I must admit, and most consistent with your assumed heritage. But don't you think perhaps a riverboat would have been more appropriate under the circumstances? More middle American, don't you know? More native."

"I never heard of an Italian riverboat," Peter protested without much enthusiasm.

But Quest had already turned his green gaze on Monica. "Bombs, my dear, were a stroke of angry genius. But had Peter been a bit more realistic, a bit more current, let us say, he could easily have countered your charge of river pollution. After all, Peter—" Quest ignored Monica momentarily, "—manufacturers of chemicals and other noxious items that make our life bearable have consistently avoided prosecution despite demonstrated thermal pollution of local waterways and massive fish kills." He turned again to Monica. "My dear, if you had been a bit more realistic, you would have hired one of the thugs who burned Miss Dear's bookstore. That way you would not have been suspected of the crime, and you would not have had to face criminal charges in court."

Tock Von, who had been listening with unbelieving ears to Quest, suddenly became alert. "Who burned the bookstore?"

"Miss Dear?" Quest said, directing Tock Von's question to her.

"Men!" she snarled. "Hundreds of them!"

"But there were no people in the Arena except us," Tock Von pointed out, indicating the group gathered about Quest.

"Nevertheless, the bookstore burned," Quest commented calmly. "That is a fact, is it not? It was a real incident, was it not? Miss Dear?"

"I saw them. Hooligans all! Banditti!"

"It was probably Pomeroy," Tock Von muttered.

Quest ignored him. "Papa Summerhall, you didn't really believe that an aspirin would help Miss Dear in her suffering, did you?"

"But it was all I had in my bag," Papa Summerhall apologized. "Next time, I'll try—" He sat down on the floor and wrapped his arms forlornly about his thin body.

Quest smiled. He reached down and patted the old man's shoulder.

"Her arm was really broken!" Tock Von said angrily.

"We'll discuss that in a moment if you wish," Quest told him. "But first Novotck, let me say that it was rather unrealistic of you not to suggest a token payment—in untraceable cash, of course—from Peter when he tried to sell you his gondolas. I'm sure, considering the excellent progress Peter has been making since coming to Excelsior, that he would immediately have recognized the wisdom of paying a stipend since you were, after all, in a position to reject his offer totally."

"What about Miss Dear's arm?" Tock Von persisted.

"We'll take Miss Dear to the dispensary. We'll take X-rays. It was most unfortunate, Miss Dear, that you chose to display *that* book in your window among the many provided by the computer program. Cookbooks would have been a safe choice. But no, you chose the very book that would be most likely to rouse the rabble. Most unrealistic, dear lady!"

"This is wrong!" Tock Von shouted. "She was *hurt!*"

"Wrong, Mr. Novotck?" Quest said. "I am not interested in either wrong or right. I am interested only in what is. I am a doctor, not a moralist or a theologian. I concern myself with things as they really are and with helping the patients in my care to comprehend that reality and adjust their behavior so that they are in harmony and not in neurotic conflict with it. No, morality is not my concern. Only reality is."

"Okay," Tock Von said. "Okay. So you're only concerned with reality. But you're operating on a typically false terrestrial premise—"

"Which is?" Quest interrupted, winking at the others who were listening to Tock Von.

"On Eleison," Tock Von said, "we wouldn't try to make one of our species conform to reality without first questioning whether or not the aspect of reality at issue was valid in terms of furthering the well-being of the Eleisonite concerned."

"How refreshingly innocent. One might almost believe, Novotck, that you had actually come from—that you really are an— But you'll learn, my friend. Although reality can be changed—until it is, a person must come to terms with it."

"No," Tock Von said firmly. "He can work to change it. He can fight it and—"

"Ah!" Quest cried, throwing up his hands in a gesture of helplessness which contained as well just the faintest tinge of contempt. "There's the rub! Neuroses arise from the very fight you were about to advocate. Psychic health may be said to be congruent with a pragmatic accommodation."

"Bullshit!" Tock Von bellowed. "The accommodation you're pushing is tantamount to slavery—a slavery of the soul."

"You speak of the soul," Quest said patiently. "It brings to mind—what would you have done in Spain during the Inquisition had you been justly or unjustly accused of heresy? Whips, remember. The rack."

"I would have—"

Quest interrupted, his eyes oddly aroused behind their green glass prisons. "You would have recanted your error. You would have knelt before the august clerics and recanted passionately, all the while praising the sweating torturer, who had so thoroughly and successfully serviced you, as a man of wisdom, one aware of the true path to enlightenment. No, wait!" Quest held up a hand to silence the argument Tock Von was about to present. "On a psychic level, it is the same. Monica, for example, for reasons best known to herself at the moment, um, has chosen to believe that she bore a child without normal phallic penetration of her vagina. Such a view obviously contradicts reality. For Monica, her belief is but a feeble defense against a reality she cannot—again for still hidden reasons—tolerate."

"It's true," Monica murmured.

Tock Von wondered if she were referring to the truth of Quest's analysis of her belief or to her claim that she had borne a child without sexual intercourse. He said to Quest, "You would make Monica kneel and recant, is that it?"

An airy wave of Quest's white hands and, "When Monica recants, so to speak—when she is at last helped to renounce her distorted view of her own behavior in relation to reality, she will be cured. She will then be able to function normally—perhaps even happily as well."

"Maybe it's better for her to believe what she believes," Tock Von said. "It certainly doesn't hurt anyone."

"It hurts her," Quest contradicted.

"No, I—" Monica immediately fell silent.

Quest said, "Reality can, admittedly, be unpleasant—quite exquisitely painful at times. For example, a person we love may die. Grief is the gift such an event gives us. Then too there are those who reject us because we are the wrong color or because they have learned to hate the things we love. But we must bear such grief if we are to mature. Otherwise, if we attempt to deny such painful elements of reality, we are doomed to remain little more than children."

"I believe in red balloons," Tock Von said. "In carousels. I believe in kindness and the fires that warm the human heart."

"Ah, but balloons burst," Quest pointed out.

"Ah, but they are lovely while they last," Tock Von countered.

"Fire can kill."

"It can also brighten a dark night."

"You must accept both the fire's light and its potential for destruction," Quest argued.

"I will not. I would prefer to teach the builders of fires to value the light they bring and to renounce the idea of the red death that lies lurking in embers."

"An impossible task," Quest observed, shaking his head.

"Not at all. A very possible task. One that should—that *must*—be undertaken."

"You are an idealist," Quest said, spitting the last word into the Arena.

"No, an Eleisonite," Tock Von said with no smile. "That's an entirely different scene. You see, what you humans preach, we Eleisonites practice."

"Hey!" shouted Chief One Wild Wolf happily. "The kid's a first class kook!" He slapped Tock Von on the shoulder in comradely fashion, causing him to cough.

"I'm not so sure," Monica said thoughtfully. "What he says makes some sense."

"But can he be trusted?" Miss Dear piped.

Tock Von had almost forgotten Miss Dear while he argued with Quest. Now, noticing her injured arm again, he said, "Quest, you carry your reality trip a bit too far."

Quest commented, "One must always and of necessity take risks within the framework of reality. Come, Miss Dear. I'll take you to the dispensary and we'll X-ray that arm."

"I cooperated," Miss Dear said, drawing away. "I really did. I even planned to open a pizza parlor—The Friends of Italy Pizza Parlor."

"I do wish," Quest whispered, guiding her toward the door, "that you had chosen to display cookbooks in your store window. No one objects to cookbooks."

"I'll bet cows do," Tock Von called out. "Chickens too. Not to mention mackerel, pheasants, deer, and pigs."

"Pure fantasy," Quest called back gaily. "None of them can read."

"What pigs don't know will hurt them," Tock Von declared.

Quest spun around, his eyes angry coins on the gaming table of his face. "You really are talking about pigs, aren't you, Novotck?"

"Pigs, yes. Like in oink-oink."

Quest glared for a moment and then turned and blinked at the door which opened in response to his flicking eyelids.

"Well," said Peter when Quest and Miss Dear had disappeared. "We made it through another session."

"I wish I could have done better," said Papa Summerhall, still sitting sadly on the floor. "But aspirin was all I had. You'd think Doctor Quest would have understood that. I'll never get out of here."

"Sure you will," Tock Von told him, helping him to his feet. "You'll get out."

"Only time will tell," Papa Summerhall said to himself. Then, with a glance at Tock Von, he added, "Have you seen my new clock?"

Tock Von said he hadn't.

Papa Summerhall promptly gripped his arm and started to drag him from the Arena. "It's really quite wonderful. Come with me."

"Not now. Later, okay?"

Papa Summerhall said, "When is later? What time precisely?"

"Tonight," Tock Von answered.

When Papa Summerhall had gone to seek his clocks, Tock Von, Monica and Peter left the Arena together and began to walk down the corridor.

"I think I'd better get back to my statistics," Peter said somewhat desolately.

"Statistics?"

Monica said, "Tock Von, Peter is compiling statistics on current war casualties. He's counting the killed."

"Grisly business," Peter admitted, scuffing along. "But someone should keep track of all the dead. You want to come and count with me, Monica?"

"Not now, Peter," she replied. "Some other time perhaps. Counting the killed depresses me, and Doctor Quest says I should avoid becoming depressed. It's bad for me, he says."

"Well, two's a crowd," Peter quipped, his fingers fidgeting erotically in his pockets. "Three's an orgy. So what do you two say?"

Mueller passed them. "One for the money," he whispered to himself, counting his currency. "Two for the money. Three for the money."

"Don't be square," Peter said to Monica. "A girl like

you has nothing to worry about. You won't have any more babies. It's against the laws of virginal probability, so don't be scared."

Monica said nothing. Tock Von said the same. Peter, shaking his head and pocketing his hands, moved away.

"How often?" Tock Von inquired of Monica. "How often do we get to take that Arena trip?"

"It's not scheduled," Monica answered. "One never knows. Doctor Quest probably has some organized plan for participation, but I haven't been able to figure it out. Sometimes we have the Arena every day for awhile and then not at all for weeks."

"I don't like it."

"None of us do, really. But it's necessary."

"Why is it necessary?"

She gave Tock Von a puzzled glance. "Why, without therapy how will we ever learn to get along out there?" She pointed to the wall beyond which lay the real world.

"Somebody broke Miss Dear's arm," Tock Von reminded her.

"I skinned my shin in the Arena one time. It was during our moon landing. I fell in a crater. Mr. Mueller hauled me out. He only charged me ten dollars for the service."

"Moon landing!"

"I don't think Doctor Quest was altogether pleased with your performance today, Tock Von."

"Neither was I. I should have found a way to prevent Miss Dear's injury."

"You really have to try," Monica said distantly. "If you don't, you'll never get out of here. You do want to get out of here, don't you?"

"Sure. I've got things to do, places to go, people to see."

"How long have you been on Earth?"

Tock Von wondered if she were teasing him. Her face—her expression was serious. No sign of a smile. She was waiting for his answer.

"Less than a week. I missed the return warp—on purpose. Little did I know what I was letting myself in for."

"What's a return warp?"

Tock Von explained the spatial theory involved in the

field trips he and the other members of the Eleisonite Expeditionary Force utilized in order to conduct their on the spot investigations into the intricacies of human behavior. When he had finished, he decided, judging by Monica's expression, that she had understood next to nothing of what he had said.

"Look at it this way," he told her. "I'm here today, gone tomorrow."

"Aren't we all," was Monica's response.

"You'd like Eleison," he said. "It's not like earth. There it's peaceful. Nobody has to hate."

She was walking a step or two ahead of him, running her hand lightly along the wall. As she came to the wide window that looked out on the grounds bordering the main lobby of the building, she placed one hip on the deep window sill and stared out. Tock Von, watching her, found himself admiring the way the sun dappled the fine bones of her face and burnished her hair. With any other girl, he would have just suggested making it. Right out. Straightforward. But Monica—well, there was something about Monica that tamed the tide of lust that rose within him at every sight of her. It was not unlike the feeling he had experienced the time he had seen a hunter drop a mallard over a lake that lay luxuriating in one more dawn. Monica was like the mallard in a way, he decided. Somewhere within her, he sensed, was a hurt that erected tall walls around her. He could scale them though, he was almost certain. He would try. But something was holding him back.

"When I get out of here," Monica said so quietly that he could barely make out her words, "I don't know what I'm going to do. I don't know where I want to go. Do you know where you'll go when you leave?"

"That depends—on a lot of things. If I were to get out of here right now, I'd probably go to India. I want to know why beggars die of starvation in the streets at night while rubies are being polished and sold not far away. Or maybe I'd find a girl and make love to her. We would talk about loneliness and broken promises."

"Are you lonely too?"

"On Eleison, there is no such thing as loneliness. Our species achieves an elemental and very rewarding kind of communication. But here—you humans—your bodies lock you away from one another. Humans are always trying to break through the barriers of their bodies to find out who it is they really love."

"Some of us are content to deal only with the barriers themselves. Some of us find it safer that way. It is a terrible thing to truly know another human being."

Tock Von was about to ask Monica exactly what she meant when Peter came bounding down the corridor and pounced upon the window sill next to Monica.

Breathless, his face flushed, he declared, "You won't believe it but it's true. No doubt about it—none! Figures don't lie."

"What is it, Peter?" Monica asked.

"Well, I told you how I've been adding up how many of our enemies have been killed in the war. I've kept a record of all the body counts—everyone. Then I called the *New York Times* and I asked them to tell me the population of our enemy's country. I couldn't figure it out at first. I rechecked my figures. No mistakes."

Tock Von listened in mild alarm as Peter began to laugh. His laughter shredded the air. It haunted the hall.

"What's wrong, Peter?" Monica asked him, evidently also sensing the ghost that stalked among them.

"We've killed them all! We've killed the entire population *two and a half times!* My figures prove it. The body counts come to a grand total of two and a half times the total population of the country!"

"There must be a mistake somewhere," Monica suggested, frowning.

"You bet there must be!" Peter almost screamed. "Killing them all just once wasn't enough for us. Hell, no! We had to do it two and a half goddam times!"

"The official figures were probably exaggerated," Tock Von said. "You can't trust them."

"Didn't I tell you?" Miss Dear said as she hopped past them, her arm in a huge cast. "Didn't I tell you that you couldn't trust *them?*"

EIGHT

"Bicycles are available upon request to authorized guests only. Interlopers are not permitted to ride."

Tock Von stood close to Monica, aware of her lush body and of his own uneleisonite response to it, as Peter ambled away, a pencil behind his ear, his sheets of paper on which Death was written in neat numerals, clutched in his angry fists.

He said nothing for a moment, feeling the physical mechanism of himself soar as Monica accidentally brushed against him on her way to the door that led to the grounds of Excelsior. He followed her, coming out into the sunshine spilling through the translucent dome, and he saw her transformed by the sun into a graceful gilded statue.

"There are bicycles," she said. "Mrs. Daley has them over there near the summerhouse. Would you like to ride?"

Tock Von, deliberately misinterpreting her question, felt himself riding on a ship of flesh whose waves enveloped him and whose soft decks he lay upon, a sailor who had found his longed for and no longer lonely harbor.

"Tock Von?"

"Sure, let's ride together." Yes, he thought, oh, yes, let's you and I ride alone together, needing no one else ever.

Mrs. Daley, when they came up to her little booth beside the stand of forsythia that bloomed wildly in yellow glory, made Monica sign an official looking form after which she wheeled out a green bicycle. Monica took it from her, thanked her.

"What about me?" Tock Von asked when Mrs. Daley began again to read from her book *The Psychodynamics of Self-Stimulation.*

"You?"

"Me."

"Name, please?"

"Tock Von."

Mrs. Daley lifted a sheet of paper and ran a finger down its list of names. "Kandor," she read. "Mueller. Novotck. Seaver. Summerhall. Sorry. We have no one by that ridiculous name on our approved list."

"But you know him, Mrs. Daley," Monica ventured. "He's—"

"Bicycles," Mrs. Daley barked, "are available upon request to authorized guests only. Interlopers are not permitted to ride."

"I'm not an interloper," Tock Von said, wondering if he were a liar.

"Then who or what are you? Your name is not on my list. See for yourself." She waved the list in front of Tock Von's face.

"There is some mistake," he told her. "Check Doctor Quest. He knows who I am."

"One moment." Mrs. Daley picked up a phone. "Doctor, Daley here. I have an unofficial person here who insists on borrowing one of our bicycles. What is the proper procedure to follow? I see. Yes, of course."

She slammed down the phone. "Mr. Novotck, you may have a bicycle, Doctor Quest says."

"I'm not Mr. Novotck. I'm Tock Von."

"No bicycle then." Mrs. Daley slammed down the steel shutter on her bicycle booth.

Tock Von turned to Monica. "It probably would have

had a flat tire anyway. You go ahead alone. Have fun. I'll wait for you here."

Monica dismounted and leaned her bicycle against the booth within which Mrs. Daley could be heard moaning in what might have been ecstasy. "We'll walk. I like to walk. Come on." She took Tock Von's arm.

They walked past the forsythia and along the prim walks and across the genteel Excelsorian lawns, letting the sun smother them with warmth.

Monica said, "It wouldn't have hurt if you'd said you were Novotck. You could have gotten a bicycle if you'd cooperated."

"Monica, what would you have done if Mrs. Daley had agreed to give you a bicycle providing you signed it out as—as Mary Malone?"

"If I wanted to ride very badly—"

"Monica, don't you see?"

"See?"

"Quest won't believe the truth I've told him. He has decided that he will impose *his* reality on me. To begin with, he has made an anagram of my name. If I accept the name he has decided to give me, what else might I not accept in time? No, I will not—"

"He's only trying to help you," Monica insisted. "He means no harm."

They were passing the delicately scrolled and whitewashed summerhouse that stood in a corner of the estate surrounded by trees and shrubbery which sheltered it from the sun. Tock Von looked at the half-open door. He went up to it and peered inside. A calico covered couch. Two chairs. He turned back to Monica.

"The sun," he said, "is hot as hell. Come on in here, okay?"

She followed him into the relatively cool interior of the refuge and sat down on one of the two chairs.

Tock Von sensed the barriers surrounding her. He heard the cry of a trumpet as he prepared to storm her battlements. But there was still that something, that wary look in her eyes that subdued his energetic, almost acrobatic, entry into the stimulating ritual of seduction. He reached out and took her hand which she let lie limply in his own.

"Lust," she remarked, "leads to disillusionment. So does love."

A strange note sounded somewhere; Tock Von heard it. "They needn't," he said quietly. "Lust and love can lead to joy." He pulled her toward him.

"No," she said without conviction. "I'm safer alone."

"Let me love you."

"You mean 'let me fuck you.' "

Tock Von saw again on the walls of his memory the mallard slicing the sun as it flew through the air, the hunter's bullet in deadly pursuit. "I want to love you, Monica."

She reached up with her free hand and touched his cheek. Her fingers, hot, brushed back the hair from his forehead, and her eyes seemed to fondle his face in search of secrets.

He rose and took her in his arms, an ache stirring within him as he felt her shudder against him. He wanted to say it. It would be so very easy to say it. It might even be true. If he said it aloud, the very saying might somehow make it true. *I love you.* But was it true? Could it be true? Or was the emotion he felt a mere biological phenomenon common to humans, one which they disguised with sweet words and small gifts in order not to face the sad fact that what drove them might not be noble at all, but simply an organic testament to the species' blind will to survive?

"I think his name was Joe," Monica said, her words nestling against his neck.

"Joe," Tock Von repeated.

"Or maybe it was Edward. He used me."

Tock Von felt her tears scald his skin. He would release her. He would sit her down and then he would sit down at a safe distance from her and he would talk to her of roses and summers. He would relinquish her. He would not force her to take risks.

But she was holding him against her, and her breasts crushed against his chest. She was making no sound as the volcano within her erupted, and the living lava of her tears declared her turmoil.

There is a time, Tock Von thought, when a human being loses himself because he cares more for another than he does for his own fleeting needs or vain goals. "Monica, let's walk. Let's walk together and—"

"But first," she said, "we must make a map for ourselves. Otherwise, we may get lost."

She drew away from him slightly, her hands resting on his biceps, her eyes on his face. She nodded slightly, seeming to listen to some distant song.

"Your name isn't Joe," she said. "It's not Edward."

He stood without moving as she began to unbutton his shirt. She moved behind him, and he positioned his arms so that she could easily slip his shirt from his shoulders. She was in front of him again and the buckle on his belt surrendered to her manipulations. When he was naked before her, he watched her slip her dress over her head. As she lifted one leg to remove her stocking, a shard of light glimmered on her calf, blinding him.

They moved to the couch together. As she knelt upon it, her hands resting on her thighs, she looked up at him and said, "Your name is Tock Von."

Gently, he heard himself warn in the cavern of his mind. Bring her an Eleisonite gentility that knows how pain can kill the person while the body walks on, talks on, and lives emptily amid death's debris.

He put his hand beneath her chin and raised her face. As he lowered his head, she closed her eyes. Their kiss was brief, their lips barely touching. Monica leaned backward and lay down upon the bed, her eyes opening to encompass the ceiling.

Tock Von lay down beside her. He placed his hand on her right breast, bringing warmth to warmth. She turned her head toward the wall.

As she did so, her hair fell over her cheek, a caul that hid her geisha's face from him.

"Monica. Let the past be only that."

There was a movement beneath his hands, a rippling of her body. No sound. Gently, he released her breast and turned her head toward him. "Open your eyes."

She obeyed him.

"It's me."

Something stirred between them. Ghosts cried out and were quickly gone as the exorcism of his honesty, which was evident not only in his expression but also in the way he touched her body, sent them howling into elsewhere.

Monica put her arms around him, drawing him closer to her. As he shuddered beneath her hot touch, she seemed to sink away from him momentarily and then she returned, another Monica, a Monica now ghostless and openly eager. She moved lithely beneath him and he entered a dimension of Earth he had never before experienced, one in which unicorns leaped and horned the sweet air, one in which seas that knew eternal strivings surged, repeating their elemental truths, now softly, now thunderously. In impossible skies, phoenixes flew in fiery rebirth. They cried out his name in Monica's voice. Tock Von and Monica, a single ship, sank into an ocean which made of drowning a rich and spiced delight.

Tock Von momentarily forgot his place in the worlds of Eleison and Earth, citizened as he now was in the mystic world of Monica. No language he knew could adequately describe its splendors. No minstrel, however inspired, could sing its bittersweet song. And bittersweet, he knew, was the song because of the inevitable and always ultimately sad arithmetic which would in time divide one into two. A feat, he thought, worthy of a darkly skilled Merlin; a task for an evil Hercules.

Monica thrust herself upward toward him as he plunged within her. They soared one wild long moment and then, their soaring giving way to a dark glide downward, held each other, Monica silent, Tock Von beyond meaningless words in the face of the fire burning his body and blinding his eyes.

An ending.

He withdrew from her and eased his body into position beside hers. Leaning on his forearm, he stared down at her face.

"I know who you are not," Monica told him.

"That's good. It's important for people to know who

other people are not. I think I know who you aren't, Monica."

"Do you think I was lying all along?"

"No. I think you had a reason for not knowing the truth. I think people always have good reasons for the lies they tell to stay alive."

"Doctor Quest says that I—"

"Monica," Tock Von interrupted, "when you are able to remember his name, the lie will die."

"He said I was the most beautiful girl he had ever seen. He gave me gifts. I remember a doll—it was a funny looking thing with bright orange hair. I think it might have been a clown. Yes, it was a clown, I'm sure of it. He said it represented the circus of ourselves in which love rode bareback and not a single clown knew how to cry. He was kind to me at first. He said he loved me. But he went away when he found out that I wouldn't have an abortion. I wanted the child—his child and mine. Marriage didn't matter. But he was so terribly afraid of the gift he had given me. It would have made him responsible."

"So you murdered him."

Monica looked sharply at Tock Von and then her face softened. She wrapped her arms around her breasts and said, "But I didn't ever hate him."

"Love kills as efficiently as hate when lovers live only within themselves."

"What about your lie?"

"Eleison?"

She nodded.

"It wasn't a lie—it isn't. Other people who will not believe my truth construct their own lies to make me fit into what is known or believed possible in their experience."

"I don't believe you."

"It doesn't matter whether you believe me or not. What matters is that we are here together now. What matters is that what has happened between us has happened. Take that and believe in it. Remember it."

"You're going away," she said, her voice flat, her body stiffening.

"Yes," Tock Von said. "In time, I must. But if human love is good, you can choose to remember me. You have risked yourself. It is the first step toward wholeness."

"*He* went away too. Everyone goes away. Life is far too full of farewells. I can't stand it!"

"The alternative, what is it? To know no one, no one at all—ever. Not in even the most minimal way. Build barricades and keep the world out. I would prefer to build strong bridges that span the distance between human hearts."

"I will not remember him. It hurts to remember him."

"Then your child will become one more lie. In time, when no other target is available, he will become your victim because he is not only yours. He will bleed as you are bleeding now. Because lies can kill."

Monica put her hands over her face. She was silent for some time. Tock Von refrained from touching her, careful to leave inches of space between the borders of their bodies. At last, she spoke.

"Stay."

"I can never really leave you now. I have crossed the bridge we built between us. Not all of me can come back to the other side—not now."

"No, I mean *really* stay with me. I need you."

"To need another person is the beginning of life. If farewells must be said, say them with sadness but don't close the door on the one leaving. Take what has been given and use it as a base on which to build a life of needing. Keep the door wide open. Let strangers come in. Learn to sing unfamiliar songs together."

Monica buried her face in the calico pillow. Her weeping was the sound of summer rain. It went on. Minutes later, her face still hidden in the pillow, she reached out to touch Tock Von. He moved close to her and let himself feel the pain that he knew was coming because there would be a goodby and he could not escape it.

At first, he was only distantly aware of the voice piercing the stillness. Lost as he was with Monica, the voice was from another world with which he had temporarily sundered contact.

"Mr. Novotck, alias Tock Von," Quest's voice buzzed into the summer house. "Report at once for a private session. Mr. Novotck, alias—"

"We have to go," Monica said nervously.

Tock Von watched her rise and begin to dress. There was, he noticed, something slightly different about her. It was not the usual languid difference, that he had witnessed often, which characterized a girl's body after the act of love. Not only that. It was that but also something more.

As they came out of the summerhouse, he realized that Monica had entered it wrapped in winter's mantle. As he watched her move carefully joyful along the walk a few steps ahead of him, he saw the first faint stirrings of spring in her stride.

"These private sessions of Quest's," he began, catching up with her. "What are they like?"

"Oh, just discussions. Doctor Quest asks questions. He talks. It's interesting."

Tock Von had his doubts but he did not declare them. He took Monica's hand, and they walked along in silence together. Miss Dear was darting among the trees near the main building, pausing behind one and then peeping cautiously out before making her dash to the safety of the next.

"There's Papa Summerhall," Monica said, waving to the old man who was riding a bicycle toward them.

"He's going too fast," Tock Von commented as he watched the bicycle come careening toward them. He released Monica's hand as the bicycle suddenly wavered and then crashed to the ground. He ran toward Papa Summerhall who was lying motionless on the ground some twenty feet up the path.

When he reached the old man, he knelt down and took his wrist where a pulse still pounded weakly. He straightened Papa Summerhall's body in an attempt to make him more comfortable and then looked up as Monica arrived on the run.

"Is he all right?" she asked.

"I'm no doctor. I don't know. I hope so."

Papa Summerhall's eyes flicked open. "What time is it? Oh, what time is it now?"

Monica glanced at her watch. "It's just past two in the afternoon. Are you hurt?"

Alarm rang in Papa Summerhall's eyes. "Yes," he said.

"What's wrong?" Tock Von inquired anxiously. "Do you think you broke any bones?"

"Don't you know?" Papa Summerhall moaned, fumbling about in his pockets and finally finding a white pill which he quickly swallowed. "It's my heart. I've been taking digoxin twice a day for years. Didn't you hear? All the clocks in the world stopped just now when I—" He put his hand on his chest. "Tick-tick?" he murmured encouragingly. "Tick?"

Tock Von helped him to his feet. "You'd better walk back."

But Papa Summerhall was paying no attention. He was gently tapping his chest with one finger, his head to one side, listening. Terror twisted the flesh of his face.

"Tock Von," Monica whispered. "He looks awful."

It was true. Papa Summerhall's face was gray and his limbs trembled.

"Please," he said. "It can't be *that* time. Not yet! Please!" He touched his chest uneasily and stared up at Tock Von. "It isn't digoxin I need. I told that to Doctor Quest. Twice, I told him. What I need is a Swiss watchmaker. A man with precise fingers and tiny tools. He could keep me running reliably."

Papa Summerhall moved gingerly away from Tock Von and Monica. He took the clocks from his pockets, one by one, and checked them for accuracy. "It's going again," he called back to them a moment later with a semblance of delight, pointing to his chest.

"He keeps all those clocks running to prove that there isn't an end to all things," Monica mused.

"You're probably right," Tock Von agreed. "He doesn't like goodbys either."

"No one does," Monica said, taking his hand again.

NINE

"Wampum isn't everything."

The first thing Tock Von noticed as he entered Quest's office was the fact that the chair which usually stood on the patient's side of the doctor's desk was missing. The second thing he noticed was the fact that the humidor from which he had taken a cigar on his first visit to the office was also missing.

He stood in front of the desk, watching Quest who was examining what looked like one of the forms Mrs. Daley had earlier carried into the Arena.

He tried to appear nonchalant, practicing the expression he had once seen a famous human movie star use as the man stood on a prairie while Indians rode the crest of a hill above him with arrows about to arch into the air. But this was no prairie, and he was no movie star, wasn't even, as a matter of Eleisonite fact, human and so such nonchalance eluded him. No one, he decided, could be nonchalant while being so thoroughly ignored and yet *present*. Nonchalance might have been possible had he been able to sit down on a chair. Or on a footstool. But standing unnoticed as he was made him feel disconnected and quite unnervingly out of it.

Should he say something, he wondered. Like, "Hey, Quest, have you heard the one about the traveling psychiatrist and the psychotic's daughter? No? Well, it seems that—"

He pressed his feet into the carpet to prove to himself that he was alive and well, well. The carpet absorbed the pressure he exerted, neutralized it, causing him to question verities.

"On your admittance form," Quest suddenly said, staring thoughtfully at his reflection in the polished surface of the desk, "you indicated that you would most like to resemble Jesus Christ. The reason you gave, as I recall, was so that you could consort freely with prostitutes. I see that you have been attempting to achieve your goal."

He couldn't dig the doctor. The witness refuses to answer, your honor.

"Monica," Quest said.

Monica? "She's not a prostitute. Hey, how did you know?"

"Our primary concern here at Excelsior is for the well-being of our patients. We monitor their behavior closely and in many ways while seeking to alter it. There is a closed circuit television system throughout the establishment. Pomeroy, during his surveillance shift, noted unusual activity in the summerhouse."

"He *watched* us?"

"He merely monitored the behavior of two patients."

"Why?"

"I've already explained why. It was not a wise thing to do, Novotck. Monica is very vulnerable."

"What was not a wise thing to do? Love her? Because she is vulnerable? Who isn't? In any reasonable society, Quest, your man Pomeroy would be brought up on charges of peeping tomism."

"Contradiction. Pomeroy would have been commended for his solicitous concern for both you and Monica."

"Did he get his jollies?"

"He is a man of good character. His concern was purely

clinical. Why did you let her seduce you? If she has another child, she may very well be driven deeper into her delusionary system in an attempt to deny what really took place between you."

"She won't have a child. We Eleisonites take precautions before our field trips. Our oil and your water don't mix, to put it in terms you'll understand."

"Stay away from Monica. When both of you have made more measurable progress—then we shall see about interpersonal dynamics. But for now—"

"Mrs. Daley wouldn't give me a bicycle."

"Mrs. Daley wouldn't give you a bicycle," Quest repeated still staring at his reflected face. "Mrs. Daley, as I understand the situation, was perfectly willing to give you a bicycle. But you refused to be *you*."

Tock Von considered sitting down on the edge of the desk as his head reeled. "She said I wasn't on her authorized list."

"She was right. You, as you insist upon defining yourself, aren't. But Novotck is."

"I don't think I want a bicycle that bad," Tock Von said a little too loudly.

"Someday—perhaps someday soon—you will want something badly enough to examine yourself in the light of our therapeutic efforts and then—ah, then you will come to your senses. Reward and punishment. A psychic teeter-totter. Up. Down. Balance is all. Novotck, there is no evidence in any government file or scientific paper to document the fact that even one being from another planet has ever visited Earth. Try to see things my way. I am a man of facts. My life's work is predicated on finding facts and teaching them to those who have chosen to ignore them. You are not Novotck admittedly—the anagrammatic nature of that name is a mere temporary convenience—but you are clearly not an extraterrestrial being either."

"I've got no fingerprints," Tock Von reminded Quest.

"As evidence of your inhumanity, missing fingerprints are inconclusive. No, my friend, you are obviously a human being."

"You're wrong. I wouldn't kill anyone either on a one-to-one basis or as part of a military machine. I don't love hate. Doesn't that prove I'm not human?"

Quest looked up finally and shook his head. "Not at all, not at all, Novotck. Your remarks merely prove your immaturity which is one of the several building blocks of your neurosis. Aggression is natural. Without it we would not be able to build giant corporations. The country's economy would collapse in its absence. Why, without aggression, our national borders would be violated with a distressing constancy. Human beings—adjusted and mature human beings—must put things in their proper place and perspective. They must compromise and accommodate. Killing in certain accepted circumstances is nothing more than duty well done. Priests praise it. They ask God to protect the soldiers they succor who do what must be done if our civilization is to survive. No, my friend, immaturity afflicts you. You really must try to let us help you. Try to understand that to love hate, as you phrased it, is but one weapon in the normal adult's arsenal with which he makes his way in an untidy world."

Tock Von studied Quest's face. The man was obviously serious. His words—they were sensible—they sounded so sane and considered. Perhaps the Eleisonite practice of loving one's neighbor and doing to him or her what good things each Eleisonite hoped to have done to him or her was faulty reasoning. Yet it did seem to work when actually and openly practiced. Perhaps the answer lay in cultural conditioning. If humans were taught slogans and subtly—almost subliminally—taught to ignore them in their pragmatic enterprises—perhaps there was after all a certain logic in Quest's remarks. The man was certainly persuasive, Tock Von realized. He sounded convincing and concerned. But, no. No! Killing served no purpose when a species-eye view of a world was taken. Tock Von shifted his weight uneasily and found himself thinking of Peter Kandor. There was hope because of the Peter Kandors who could not kill. But was there really? The Peter Kandors of Earth, Tock Von thought with something akin to despair, filled places like Excelsior. They occupied jail cells because they had set up the god of personal conscience on the stained altar of legitimate authority. Then could—?

"Novotck, I *care!*"

Tock Von crashed off his thoughtful track. The despair he had sensed lurking in his thoughts suddenly loomed before him. It was true. Quest did care. He cared enough to harbor renegades of all types, and his caring was a smile on the face of love that hid from the smiler himself all the confusions and death rattles of strangled doubts.

"Look at it this way," Quest was saying. "If you really were an alien, this world would have no place for you. You would be ostracized. You would be invisible. You have much to offer to the world—to *our* world. You are not an insensitive young man. You have a good mind despite its presently clouded character. Don't be afraid to be yourself. Tell me what it is that has so frightened you and caused you to retreat into this defensive fantasy of Eleison and alienation."

Tock Von took a quick step backward. "I guess I appreciate your concern and like that. But I don't need any help. Thanks just the same, but—"

"The first step toward health is the admission of sickness," Quest said. "Let me get you a chair."

He rose and went to a door. He opened it and went through it. When he returned, he was carrying a chair. He placed it behind Tock Von and clapped one heavy hand on Tock Von's shoulder, pushing him down into the chair.

Tock Von remembered the cocktail party and his deliberate avoidance of the return warp. *Smartass,* he told himself in the morass of his mind. Smartass Eleisonite, you paid your money and what happened? Quest is making your choices, that's what. The chair beat his buttocks.

"Comfortable?"

"Uh—"

"Good." Quest leaned back in his chair that seemed to fondle his fatness. "We do not usually favor any of our guests because it tends to disrupt the always delicate interpersonal harmony we seek to achieve. But in your case, Novotck, I think protocol can be safely suspended temporarily."

"Don't," Tock Von said, holding up a hand. "Don't—"

"The Arena will open in a few minutes, and you will once again have an opportunity to relinquish your distorted ideas of what is real and what is merely a crutch to aid the cripple in his flight from reality. Can you picture it, my friend? A cripple fleeing on his crutches? Would it not be far better were he to stand up on his own two strong feet with no artificial aids to his equilibrium—no crutches or debilitating symptoms of mistaken identity?"

"My identity is not mistaken!" Tock Von responded angrily. "Not by me, it isn't! You mistake it! Quest, you can't see the person for the symptoms. You mistake Peter's love for living people for an aberration when it's nothing more than ordinary decency. You think Monica is sick because she won't remember the name of the cat who balled her and then cut out when she got pregnant. Why should she remember his name? Why should Peter be called sick because he put a bullet in his foot in order to avoid murdering someone?"

"Sane people don't shoot themselves," Quest declared. "Adjusted women accustom themselves to the pain of betrayal. Novotck, you accuse me of making mistakes. Ironic, considering the grandest mistake of all which you are making concerning who you really are."

"I'll make a deal with you," Tock Von said. "I'll take you to the locus of the return warp. You can watch me move, man. Like right out of this world of yours—and I mean literally."

"I think—yes, it is definitely time for another session in the Arena. You are clearly in desperate need of reality orientation. Perhaps you are not yet willing to admit to the fears which prevent you from facing the fact that you are human but— Well, that can wait a bit. An attack on peripheries may be the best route to a cure."

"Peripheries? Quest you talk like a goddam cryptographer."

Quest ignored the remark. "Peripheries, yes. If you can learn to deal with the specifics of the programed environments in the Arena, then perhaps your major defense mechanism will disintegrate in the learning process and you will then be able to truly know yourself. An example. A child likes the feel of his oatmeal. He flings it at the wall to make mushy patterns. Such a child soon learns that oatmeal must be eaten if he is to live. That elementary fact, once learned, places the child vis-a-vis his oatmeal in a harmonic reality relationship. Novotck, you will learn to eat your oatmeal. You *will* be well. I promise you."

"I promise you, Quest, that I will be only me."

"That will be all for now. Immediately after lunch, we will open the Arena. Within its walls you will have an opportunity to test the real world and your relationship to it."

Tock Von became aware of the tension in his legs. He turned and went to the door which opened in response to his very first blink. He went through it and slammed it behind him.

"Ooooo!"

"Miss Dear!" he exclaimed, surprised to find the lady lying on her back on the floor. "What—?"

"I was listening!" she cried, scrambling to her feet with Tock Von's help. "I *heard!*"

"Here, let me help you fix that sling." Tock Von adjusted the sling covering the cast on Miss Dear's arm which had slipped off when the opening door had sent her sprawling.

"Young man, he's one of them. I haven't the slightest doubt. Beware!"

"Quest?"

"I told you I heard every word. He's working for the AEC. Did I ever tell you about the AEC?"

"Yes, you told me that the American Education Committee was spying on you and the members of your organization."

"We are not, however, subversive unless subversion is a word that can be applied with impunity to girls like us who want freedom now. But about Doctor Quest—I know he's one of them. If you know how to listen to what he says—not the words he speaks but their *meaning*—then it all becomes perfectly clear. That matter of the child and the oatmeal—clearly a code. You had better watch out, young man. I'm certain that he was sending secret signals to Senator Sturm of the AEC. They've undoubtedly got your number now too."

Tock Von suppressed the laughter that seethed within him. "Then that makes us co-conspirators, Miss Dear."

She looked over her shoulder. She raised her fist in the air and shook it about. Tock Von immediately imitated her gesture.

"We've just got to get out of here," she whispered. "Sometimes when I'm in the Arena I get quite addled. I live in fear that I shall lose my mind. I never ran a bookstore in my life. But Doctor Quest—he made me. I'm not a bookstore owner. I'm a *woman!*"

"I'm on your side," Tock Von whispered in what he hoped was his most conspiratorial tone. "We'll beat him at his own game. After all, you and I have our own code, don't forget that."

The anxiety began to disappear from Miss Dear's features. It was replaced by a smile that brought a sigh in its wake. "Bless bless you you, young young man man."

Tock Von was not prepared for the way she sprang upon him. The kiss she delivered to his cheek was as dry as a desert, a souvenir of the Sahara of her life, but it was nonetheless passionate as kisses between conspirators, he guessed, should always be.

"Chief One Wild Wolf," she confided to him. "He plans to smuggle out a letter which will save us all from *him!*" She pointed to Quest, invisible behind the door of his office. "The letter points out that the land on which Excelsior rests rightfully belongs to the Indian tribes who make up the Iroquois nation. He insists that Doctor Quest be forced to surrender it to its original owners from whom it was stolen long ago."

"Who's he sending the letter to?"

"Why, to the Sierra Club, of course. They're conservationists. The Chief bases this, his latest plea, on the premise that the Indians should be conserved as a natural national resource. His motto is, 'Conserve, don't reserve.' A reference to the reservations, you know."

Tock Von raised his fist a second time in response to Miss Dear's determined gesture, and they parted.

As he walked toward the cafeteria where, Mrs. Daley was declaring over the intercom system, dinner was waiting, he found himself amused at Miss Dear's ability to find plotters everywhere. It seemed to him that with so many plotters populating her world, there was hardly anyone left except herself to plot against. There was, however, some truth in what she said, he decided. While Quest might not be a member of the AEC, he was definitely of the same ilk as its members. Quest, like the members of the AEC, sought to identify and correct subversives. Miss Dear, the Chief, Peter, even Monica—they were all subversives who had topsy-turvied the normal order of things and were therefore worthy of the attention of a Doctor Quest who valued order above disorder, highways above detours. Miss Dear, then, was right in her way.

In the cafeteria, Tock Von looked around and found Monica seated with Chief One Wild Wolf. At a table nearby, Peter sat with a disconsolate chin in one hand, staring with forlorn eyes at Monica.

"Is three a crowd, as I've heard it said on Earth?" Tock Von asked as he came up to Monica and the Chief.

"Sit down," the Chief said. "We're having a war council."

"Hi," Monica said.

Tock Von, instead of answering, smiled at her. He wanted to reach out and touch her, but it really wasn't necessary. They were touching. He felt it. Their touch was tactile with smiles and memory.

"Chief One Wild Wolf," Monica informed Tock Von, "intends to make trouble for Doctor Quest. I wish he wouldn't."

"Miss Dear told me about your letter," Tock Von said to the Chief. "It's worth a try."

"Damn right," agreed the Chief heartily. "I'm going to keep at it until all territories occupied by the Indian's enemy are liberated."

"That's an unrealistic attitude," Monica said.

The Chief frowned at her. "You keep it up and Quest will make you a staff member. You're starting to sound just like him."

"I think we should all try to cooperate with him. He's trying to help us, after all."

"Monica," Tock Von said, "he's laying a bad scene on us all—especially in the Arena. If we learn to do his thing, we'll soon forget how to do our own. We won't be *us* anymore."

"The kid's right," the Chief said, nodding vigorously. "Quest and his Reality Indices are just another white man's game to subdue the enemy—in this case, *us* the enemy."

"That's exactly my point," Tock Von said, addressing Monica directly.

"Quest," the Chief went on, "as my corrupted brethren say in all the white western movies, speaks with a forked tongue. When he raps, only snakes listen."

"But if we cooperate with him," Monica argued, "we'll get well. We'll also get out of here."

"She's got a point," the Chief said to Tock Von. "Maybe we should play the old bastard's game. Maybe the end we all want justifies the means we take to achieve it. What do you say, kid?"

"All I can say is that Quest is wasting his time with me. It's a bit different with the rest of you. But I still believe that he's working from a false premise. He can't see—or he won't see—that reality isn't necessarily always good. He doesn't emphasize the chance to change reality. That's what puts us all on one side and him on the other. We've changed reality to suit ourselves so we've got to be brought back into line. Right, left, and forward march!"

A tray crashed to the floor near the end of the cafeteria line.

"It's Mr. Mueller," Monica said, rising. "What's the matter with him?"

Tock Von watched Mueller as he stood, his hands at his sides, staring down at the tray he had dropped as if he hoped to find in the goulash of mashed potatoes, black-eyed peas, and boiled chicken wings an answer to great questions.

"He's freaked out," the Chief commented. "It happens. The guy looks like somebody just shot his best friend."

Tock Von rose from the table. "I'll be right back," he said and moved toward Mueller. When he reached the man, he had to speak his name twice before Mueller responded. The response, when it came, was weak. Mueller raised his eyes and stared at something just beyond Tock Von's left shoulder. Tock Von put a hand on Mueller's shoulder and gently guided him away from the minor disaster at his feet. Under the disapproving frown of Pomeroy at his spoon counting station and past the diminishing glare of Mrs. Daley who was making a surreptitious note on a napkin, Tock Von led Mueller.

When he had eased him into a chair next to Monica, he said, "You're among friends, Mueller. If you want to talk about it, we'll listen. If you don't, fine."

"My money," Mueller said softly, counting on his fingers. "Ten thousand, eleven, twelve— All gone. I just had a private session with Doctor Quest. He helped me to see that—he helped me to understand that without my money, I'm nothing. He showed me my emptiness. He said he had to do it before he could help me find something else to fill up the emptiness. But I don't want anything else! Nothing matters to me now. Doctor Quest explained that I'm a masochist. He said that's why I gave away all my money—a twenty dollar bill here, a thousand dollar check there."

"Wampum isn't everything," the Chief said sympathetically.

"You'll make more," Monica said in an attempt to alleviate Mueller's pain, which manifested itself in a fat tear that oozed from his left eye.

"I don't want to," Mueller said. "Don't you understand?"

Tock Von watched the tear descend the hill of Mueller's cheek and careen wetly down to drip from his chin onto his white shirt where it left a gray stain.

Mueller swallowed and said, "The money was all I had to show for all the years. I was so busy making it that I didn't have time to live. With each dollar I gave away, I gave away part of myself—all I ever was. That's what Doctor Quest told me."

"The sonofabitch!" the Chief snarled, munching on a carrot.

"He said," Mueller continued, "that the real reason I gave my money away was so that the people I gave it to would lu-lu-love me."

Monica watched in fascination as Mueller's moan rose, an insect on a droning flight, until it reached a shrieking crescendo.

Chief One Wild Wolf quietly cursed the white man's medicine.

Tock Von sat still, overwhelmed by a sense of helplessness in the face of Mueller's inner agony, as Mueller shuddered his way at last into a stricken silence.

TEN

"Wait! What about me? Who am I?"

Through the Excelsiorian halls rang the Arena's summoning chime, damming Mueller's tears, raising Chief One Wild Wolf to his feet, wrenching a sigh from Monica, and angering Tock Von who was wishing he knew some earthly way to stop fools like Quest, who wittingly placed banana peels in the paths of cripples.

Miss Dear dashed past their table, pausing only long enough to give Tock Von a raised fist and a secret message which he failed to decipher.

Papa Summerhall wound his Superman watch, shook his railroad watch vigorously, glanced up at the clock above the steam tables, and called out in a metronome's voice that everyone had better hurry or else they'd all be irrevocably late.

"Tock Von," Monica said, "you look so angry. Don't make any trouble. Cooperate with Doctor Quest. You'll only hurt yourself otherwise."

He was about to reply to Monica's admonition, but the words he had been about to hurl at her would, he realized, mean next to nothing to her, since she was still so earnestly seeking to cooperate with Quest and his therapeutic folderol in the Arena. Cooperate, he thought. A slippery word, not unlike such others as expediency and adjustment. He thought back over his research into human history. He thought of all the good Germans who had so thoroughly, in true Germanic tradition, cooperated with the fanged and clawed authority that had one day crawled out of some dank jungle to control their lives. He thought of how some of the good citizens of that once more young Reich had actively welcomed the jungle's law and of those others, more evil and therefore more pitiable, who had cooperated by closing their eyes and their minds to windows smashed by boys high on hate, and to yellow-starred citizens required by Reichian law to step down into the gutter when jolly burghers walked possessively about on Aryan sidewalks.

Cooperation, large and small, from midnight to midnight, had wiped away six million criminals whose common crime was an accident none of them had been able to control because birth was as arbitrary as death, and neither was manageable by the individual most concerned.

Monica took his hand and hope awoke in him. Had she not refused to cooperate in her love's betrayal? Such a girl could not live forever in the boundless mire of cooperation, because such a girl had learned to say no to an evil who walked on his hind legs and barked loudly about love, while remaining safely within his own irresponsible orbit. Yes, there was hope for Monica. Burning from the touch of her hand, Tock Von accompanied her out of the cafeteria, confident that this girl to whom he was now linked by something far stronger than interlocked fingers had her limits which, once she had identified them, she would not go beyond.

"Hurry!" Papa Summerhall called out, his thumb poised above the button on the stopwatch he held in his hand. "Monica, my dear, and Tock Von—*hurry!*"

As he entered the Arena with Monica, Tock Von immediately looked up to where Quest was already seated in his tiny balcony, beaming down with pleasure at the assembling patients. Pomeroy was in his usual position in front of the huge face of the computer. Mrs. Daley, wearing a wilting rose in her unkempt hair, shuffled her forms impressively under Quest's encompassing eye.

"Ready?" Quest called down.

Papa Summerhall brought his thumb down on his stopwatch.

"In our modern world," Quest announced from his balcony, "education is a commodity that few of us can afford to do without. Education enables some of us to sell deodorant effectively. It allows others to analyze the cost overrun factors on defense contracts. For still others like myself, it reveals the mysteries of the human mind. It unravels the mysteries of the internal combustion engine, it tells us why tadpoles turn into frogs, it highlights history, magnifies our understanding of the stars—yes, education is the key with which we unlock the doors of mysteries and make sense out of chaos.

"All this, ladies and gentlemen, is but a prelude, a mild introduction, to the new program I have constructed for the computer and which will be physically manifested in the Arena momentarily. Musing recently, as is my occasional custom, on the merits of education and realizing that education is the solid cornerstone of the magnificent edifice of life, I have decided to let you all participate in the educational process for your individual benefits. The fact that some of you have not had extended formal education will in no way hinder your functioning. It will, rather, challenge those of you less endowed to be more imaginative, more creative. For those of you who have been educated at higher levels, the experience will prove somewhat familiar but, I trust, not dull. Improvising, you see, is all.

"Now we are all familiar with the routine, are we not? Then let me welcome you, ladies and gentlemen, to the lovely campus of Universal University. But a few pertinent facts first. The University receives no government support but is dependent upon the generosity of its alumnae and Bond Mueller, in this little drama, is an alumnus of UU."

A numb Mueller nodded assent.

"The University," Quest went on, "teaches what should

be known. It is considered conservative-liberal. It has always had a relationship with the town in which it is situated. It will be up to all of you to determine the precise nature of that relationship, of course. UU's motto is: MIND! With an exclamation point. Monica, you will be an Assistant Professor. As such, I might mention, you will be considered successful but not too or entirely successful. After all, only full professors are truly successful—if not quite contented always. Chief One Wild Wolf is UU's Chancellor. Miss Dear—please pay attention to me, Miss Dear—you are the Dean of Women, a thoroughly challenging position in today's world of the pill and pop liberation. Papa Summerhall is a graduate student, how typical remains to be seen. Novotck, you will be an undergraduate student. You may select your own major once the drama begins. Now then, are we all ready?"

Peter yelled, "Wait! What about me? Who am I?"

Quest shook his head in chagrin, apologized to Peter for having forgotten him and consulted his notes. "Yes, here it is. Peter, you have a quite deliciously provocative role this time. You are UU's Head Custodian and, I should add, black. Pomeroy!"

Pomeroy turned to the computer. *Flick, switch, push, press!*

Mrs. Daley opened the lid of the enormous trunk and began tossing costumes onto the floor.

Papa Summerhall seized a tweed sportcoat and a briar pipe. Monica, a drab woolen dress. Miss Dear rummaged through the trunk and came up with a tailored suit suprisingly emblazoned on each lapel with a bright red U. The others selected clothes they deemed appropriate as reinforcements for their temporary identities and managed to change into them without sacrificing either modesty or speed.

Tock Von dodged nimbly out of the way of descending ivied walls as the brass voice of the bell in the school's old clock tower began to ring, deafening him and delighting Papa Summerhall. Looking up at the stone facade of the building taking shape before him, he saw the single word MIND! spelled out in miniature electric light bulbs. It flashed on, flashed off, on again. Quest vanished along with his balcony behind a sports stadium that ballooned up out of the floor complete in every detail, but minus the usual cheering mob which, Tock Von had learned, liked to do vicarious battle on artificial turf via the muscled bodies of their often all too temporary heroes.

"Monica," he yelled as she began to move away from him.

She didn't turn. He called her name a second time. She looked back over her shoulder and said, "Were you speaking to me?"

"Who the hell else is named Monica around here?" he shouted at her.

"My name is Miss Ventnor. I do think it would become you to observe simple proprieties."

Tock Von stared at her. "Okay! So okay, dammit! I'm majoring in—what's your department, Miss Ventnor?"

"Biology."

"I'm majoring in biology. Teach me all I need to know."

Peter came sweeping past, a broken broom in his hands. He looked at Monica, groaned, and leaned defeated on his broom.

"My class begins in—" Monica glanced at her watch, "—in five minutes. Today we will dissect a cat."

"I wish I could afford the tuition," Peter muttered to Tock Von. "I'd sure like to have a chance to dissect her pussy."

Monica Miss Ventnored away in a woolen huff.

"Hey," Peter said to Tock Von, "you know what the trouble with her is? I'll tell you. She needs variety to spice up her life. Now you take a black guy like me—I could be just what she needs. What she needs, as I see it, is a cock of a different color."

Tock Von laughed despite the anger that was still surging within him. Let Quest try his best, he thought. He was doomed to failure. Telling Peter he was black and a school custodian in no way altered Peter's basic sexual orientation. Out it came, a stream of sexy consciousness that could not be dammed.

"I say," said Papa Summerhall to Tock Von from his studious position at the base of a bepigeoned statue of Disraeli. "I say, young man, you wouldn't happen to have the time, would you?"

Tock Von told him what time it was.

"No, you misunderstand me. I was talking about whether or not you think a person might possibly have the time to learn all the things there are to be learned in these books." He patted the thick red and blue volumes under his arm. "I've been at it for more years than I can count and I still don't know enough."

"It takes time," Tock Von told him, amused.

"You know something," Papa Summerhall declared with some excitement. "You're a very profound young man. You must be majoring in chronology."

"Nope. Biology. Me and Miss Ventnor, we share a deep interest in biology."

"Chronology's important," Papa Summerhall insisted. "Time consuming though."

Tock Von walked in the direction Monica had taken, looking for some sign of Pomeroy and his computer, for the chameleon presence of Mrs. Daley, for the supervisory balcony of Quest. None of them were visible although he thought he caught a glimpse of Pomeroy through the stone archway separating the men's and women's dormitories. But it was only Chief One Wild Wolf polishing the brass plate on an iron gate which read WELCOME TO UNIVERSAL UNIVERSITY WHERE MEETINGS OF MINDS MATTER.

And, in small raised letters underneath, a sly reminder: *Courtesy of Everest Quest, M.D.*

He walked on into the building in search of Monica and finally found her behind a lectern in an empty classroom. He seated himself and opened the blank blue book he found on his desk.

"—and the creatures," Monica was saying, "reproduce without sexual intercourse. The process is called fission and takes place in all such self-fertilizing mature organisms. It has a number of very interesting aspects among which are—"

Tock Von raised his hand.

"Yes, Mr. Novotck?"

He wasn't quite sure what he intended to say but he wanted to shatter the genteel air of complacency that pervaded UU and which had evidently infected Monica as well.

"You have a question, Mr. Novotck?"

"No, a cause."

"Amoeba and paramecia are only two examples of one-celled animals which—"

"What this place needs is a good revolution," Tock Von interrupted. "Amoeba aren't relevant to where students' heads are at. I speak for togetherness. Let's you and me get it together, Miss Ventnor. Long live the revolution!"

"Hold it!" Mueller yelped, leaping into the classroom. "There will be no revolutions in the University I own! I donate a goodly number of dollars every year to this place, and so I call the classes. Revolution is not now and never will be a part of the approved curriculum."

Monica hastily gathered up her notes and stepped from behind the lectern.

Where, thought Tock Von, are you Quest? Can you see the match in my hand? Can you foresee the flames I will ignite that will bring your phony trip down to the ground?

"Miss Dear!" Mueller was bellowing, his hands cupped around his mouth. *"Miss Dear!"*

In she came, her eyes wary, her feet prancing. "What is it? What's wrong, Mr. Mueller?"

"Spies!" Mueller shouted. "Radicals and revolutionaries are at large. My money is being perverted in the cause of creeping Communism. The capitalistic system is under siege. Seize her!"

"Miss Ventnor?" Miss Dear gasped. "Who's she been spying on?"

"Get her out of here. Him too." Mueller gesticulated, his face reddening. "I've seen her somewhere before. She had bombs in her hand at the time, as I recall. Her talk about paramecia is merely a cover for insidious plans."

"Oh, I just knew it!" Miss Dear wailed. "They are everywhere. But until now I never suspected biology! Miss

Ventnor, come with me to my office. I will call Chief Chancellor Wolf and he will prepare the necessary forms which, once you have signed them, will insure your loyalty."

"Miss Dear—" Monica ventured.

"She's an undercover agent," Tock Von told Miss Dear as he pointed at Monica. "Not to be trusted."

Miss Dear gasped and flew from the classroom.

Mueller snorted, triumphant.

As Monica ran from the room, Tock Von ran after her. He caught up with her outside the building and was about to take her arm and turn her around to face him when Miss Dear's voice shrilled, splitting the dry educational air.

"They are destroying the very foundations of—"

"The free enterprise system," Mueller shouted as he came out of the building.

"They are destroying," continued Miss Dear undaunted, her voice a kite on a wild wind, "the very fine moral fabric of America. They are a cancer on the body societal. They must be stopped!"

Papa Summerhall, roused from his slumber at the foot of Disraeli's statue, leaped up to join a crowd of plastic figures wearing blazers and beanies. "It is time for all good men to come to the aid of their country!" he screeched.

Chief One Wild Wolf appeared from the cafeteria to plead for calm and a chance to reason together. He came up to Tock Von and muttered, "Just what the hell's going on here?"

"Revolution," Tock Von replied. "UU is irrelevant."

"This is hallowed ground," the Chief said sternly. "Scholars have nourished it with their dissertations. Academicians have filled its sacred air with theories and intelligent cant. Besides which, it's private property and nobody's going to take it away from me."

Mueller rose up on his toes and announced, "Not another dollar, Chancellor. Not one red cent—I mean, not a cent unless—"

Miss Dear fell silent at the sound of the word "red."

"Teach truths," Mueller ordered everyone. "Speak of geometric progressions and Thorstein Veblen. Let the walls of UU resound with Aristophanic laughter. Rout out all unbelievers in the law and order of supply and demand, cash and carry!"

The great bell in the clock tower began to strike an hour.

At the same instant, Papa Summerhall began to fidget as the clocks he had secreted in the pockets and pouches of his clothes raised their own voices to create a chorus of chimes, chirps, clicks and carols to mark the demise of one more hour. The tempo of Papa Summerhall's fidgeting slowed at one o'clock when the silent minute hand moved on into the new hour. He called out to Peter, who was stalking Monica past the locked glass display case in the quadrangle in front of the Student Union, the display case which contained the rifles used by UU's championship Gun Club. "Boy," he called loudly, "we're an integrated army. No discrimination or other untimely tragedies mar the minds of our brave boys. Boy, UU wants you!"

Peter paused briefly in his stalking and then leaped. But Monica managed to evade him. She hurried back to where Tock Von was standing beside Mueller.

As she arrived, Mueller slipped into the Student Union and emerged a few minutes later carrying an empty soda bottle and some paper napkins. He ran toward his white Mustang that was parked at the edge of the quadrangle.

"Fight fire with fire!" he roared a moment later, brandishing the no longer empty soda bottle in his hand—the soda bottle he had filled with gasoline quickly siphoned from his Mustang's tank. "Long live the American way of pay as you go!"

"Tock Von," Monica said nervously, gripping his arm. "Mr. Mueller is—"

Tock Von didn't hear the rest of her sentence because he was running toward Mueller who was striking matches in a fit of what could only be called ecstasy, judging by the man's beatific expression. *"Mueller!"* Tock Von called out as he ran toward him. As he turned to find the source of the shout, one of Mueller's matches flared brightly and the paper napkins he had stuffed into the throat of the soda bottle burst into flame.

Peter was kicking the case containing the rifles and dodging the flying glass that resulted from his assault.

"Back, Mueller!" he yelled, raising a rifle. "Us down home black folks have got to protect the little bit we got from you white entrepreneurs and other honky hustlers. Your money just don't talk our funky language. Back!"

But Mueller, as Tock Von stood momentarily paralyzed between him and Peter, raised his torch, a blazing beacon.

"I bought and paid for it!" Mueller screamed, waving his arms at the buildings that were Universal University. "I will not let a revolting world take it all away from me."

Peter raised his rifle and fired a warning shot.

The torch tore through the air and smashed in a mass of flame against the Arts and Sciences Building.

"Stop the idiot!" Chief One Wild Wolf yelled, kicking a futile foot at the flames that were seeking to eat the simulated granite wall of the building.

Another shot.

Tock Von felt himself turning, felt his mind making ugly adjustments so that he would be prepared to face whatever he might see when he had completed his revolution and was facing Mueller. . . . It took him years to turn. It took additional eons for his eyes to accept the fact of Mueller's fallen body. A torn place in the man's neck was letting loose a red rain to feed the grass.

"No!" Monica screamed too late.

Tock Von was vaguely aware of Miss Dear standing alone in a thick silence. He could not see her face. He could not see her bird's body. Only her broken arm in its white hammock was visible to him.

Papa Summerhall was kneeling beside Mueller, holding both of the man's wrists and counting. . . .

"Tick. Tick. He's still—"

"Peter!" Tock Von shouted.

Peter lowered the rifle he was holding. He stared at it and at his hands that held it. His head moved slowly from side to side in a futile attempt to deny, to negate the distance he had traveled in the journey which he had not known he was embarking upon when the drama in the Arena began another existence ago.

The people in the Arena stood out in crystalline clarity as Tock Von's gaze moved from one of them to the next and on. Miss Dear, touching her arm and whining as if she were being struck by a delicately painful whip. Papa Summerhall, counting the minutes that moved toward an end. Chief One Wild Wolf standing helplessly, entranced by the evil spell of spilled blood. Monica, slumping to the ground, her limbs liquid, her eyes tightly closed. Mueller, staring dully up in search of death. And Peter, stunned into immobility, the rifle riveted to his hands, its butt finding a comfortable resting place against his groin, its barrel pointing stiffly skyward.

Quest.

Tock Von saw him emerge from the Arts and Sciences Building. He felt a very human rage rise within him as the fat man in the green glasses came hurrying toward the people in the Arena. They were puppeting now toward one another, sheeping together in search of a safety that would deny the fact of death and give them a wooly strength that would sustain them through one more day of time and the changes time brought.

Tock Von's hands formed fists as he bent down over the dying Mueller.

Quest asked questions.

If Mueller heard them, he did not respond to them. Instead, he stared at Tock Von.

"You—" he sighed. "We are all aliens, my young friend. We—" The sound of a sluggish river sounded in his throat, temporarily drowning his words. "We try to find our way to each other but there are—detours. Peter—"

"I thought," Peter said, "that it wasn't loaded."

A damp laugh from Mueller. "No matter. No matter now. But Peter—I must tell you before I—Peter, the guns we fire at one another are always loaded."

"You killed him!" Tock Von heard himself shout at Quest in a voice that was totally unfamiliar to him. Even as the words ripped from his lips, he wondered why it mattered. What were these humans to him—to an Eleisonite who had come to Earth and would one day be gone? Who was Bond Mueller but another anthropoid specimen worthy only of some brief speculation, a bit of Eleisonite amusement, a goodby?

"An accident," Quest said, turning from Mueller to stare up at Tock Von.

Tock Von watched his hands rise and reach out. He marveled at the expertise with which they seized and circled Quest's throat. He found it almost boring to watch them sink firmly into the folds of flesh garlanding Quest's neck.

But then he felt his fingers being unlocked. Pomeroy's own sudden hands were the keys with which the lock of his own was released. He found himself pinioned by Pomeroy as Quest placed a clean linen handkerchief over the weak geyser in Mueller's throat that no longer pumped so vigorously and then closed first one and then the other eye to bring an end to Mueller's empty world.

"He's dead," Quest said flatly.

"You murdered him," Tock Von accused.

"Not so," came Quest's response. "His death was an accident. He should have evaluated the potentially revolutionary situation much more realistically. It was likely—indeed highly probable—that the rifle Peter used in an attempt to protect the property of his employer was loaded with live ammunition. No, Mueller's death was due to his faulty reality orientation. It was, as I've said, accidental.

"I shall prepare a report for the county coroner which will absolve Excelsior and its staff—not to mention Peter—from any responsibility for the unfortunate incident. Mr. Novotck, it would be good for you if you can bear in mind that reality, as I've said previously, is not always pleasant. Coping with it always involves risks. In the microcosmic universe of the Arena, risks are always present just as they are—outside."

Peter said, "I didn't mean to do it. But it seemed to be the right thing to do at the time. He had a molotov cocktail. I saw it. Somebody had to stop him."

"Precisely," Quest said, placing a hand on Peter's faintly trembling shoulder. "Peter, you acted realistically and for that I commend you. There is really nothing more that I can do for you. Excelsior has nothing more to offer you in your pursuit of health."

Peter looked up in dismay. "You mean that I—?"

"I do. Mrs. Daley will prepare the proper forms within the hour. You will then be released."

Peter leaned his head against the barrel of his rifle and moaned.

As Quest turned toward him, Tock Von fought to free himself from Pomeroy's grip.

Quest said, "An isolation room, Pomeroy. Our Mr. Novotck does seem quite agitated."

Tock Von called to Monica, something about limits, and she ran toward him, her hands reaching out for him. But Quest captured her arm and pulled her back as Pomeroy lifted Tock Von and carried him from the Arena.

ELEVEN

"Here on Earth, we weep."

"So okay," Tock Von told the walls of the isolation room on the second day of his confinement within it. "Quest is queer for reality. So okay. Point: Reality is not an absolute which is Quest's first false step. Point: No fencer expects to be killed with his own foil."

Hey, nonny, nonny and voilà!

One of the wall's two foot square segments neoned into life. Red fluorescence said: FOOD. Another, higher up and to the right, glowed bluely to life: FRIEND. A voice sounding like Quest's but without the vague under-edge of unctuousness intoned, "The patient is welcome to play another game of Priorities. The palm of the patient's hand, when pressed to the selected square, will record in descending order of preference said patient's priorities and indicate, incidentally and importantly, patient's progress to date. Player-Patient's move, please."

Tock Von watched the chessboard of the wall wink wildly at him in slick Questian words.

SEX. WARMTH. POMEROY. FLOWER. And in yellow neon bordered in orange: REALITY.

Scylla, he thought. Charybdis. The River Styx. Oh, Charon, where are you now that I need you? A deep laugh which began and ended in his simulated human gut. A wink of a wary eye at no one and a palm up against the word LOVE. Another against the name POMEROY.

The unctuous voice again. "Does the patient find difficulty coping with homosexual impulses? Does he/she desire reorientation in appropriate sexual directions?"

How to talk to a machine?

"Follow the rules, please. Indicate preferences by palming verbal symbols to convey personal impulses. Patient is politely requested to (A) refrain from speaking aloud, and (B) to work within the system of the game. Proceed."

Tock Von unpalmed the word LOVE. He kept his palm, which was growing moist beneath the onslaught of hot neon, on the name POMEROY. He managed, by contorting his body into an impossible position, to place his free hand on the word REALITY.

The machine clicked briefly and then said, "Does the patient wish to identify with the staff member designated in an attempt to integrate his behavior into the reality represented by the named authority figure?"

Tock Von opened his mouth to speak but promptly shut it as more squares lighted up: NO, YES, MAYBE, NONE OF THE ABOVE, PATIENT PASSES.

He quickly placed both palms on the word YES.

"Patient will proceed to Reinforcement of Priorities Phase."

Tock Von repeated his choices and contortions until the machine's voice fell silent.

When all the lights in the wall had gone out, murdering the words, he waited. While he waited, he thought about Mueller's body lying bloodied on the floor of the Arena. He thought of Monica and how his own extraterrestrial love could bring pain in the very same degree that mundane love can. Miss Dear tripped through his thoughts, avoiding spies with every anxious step, and Papa Summerhall talked of clocks and how nothing could happen without them because events could not possibly occur in a state of timelessness. Chief One Wild Wolf stole a Tock Vonian thought, claiming it rightfully belonged to him since he had thought it first. But it was Monica who kept returning, now near, now far away, as she searched through her own neural connections and mental congruities for the lost name of a lying love, almost completely forgetting Tock Von in the earnest process.

"I am told," announced Quest, unexpectedly beaming his way into the white room, "that you are quite calm now and in need of some realistic diversion."

"How come you let guns with live ammo in them be part of the Arena program?" Tock Von demanded.

"You are thinking of Mr. Mueller's unfortunate accident. Let me put it this way, Mr. Novotck. There were cars in the Arena the first time you participated. One of you, as events unfolded, could conceivably have been struck by one of those cars. Guns, automobiles, household cleaning fluids—all are potentially lethal. But do you think any medical examining board would find me guilty of misconduct because I included ammonia in the kitchen of one of the Arena scenes and someone drank it?"

"You should eliminate such things. You know that your patients might do something rash sometimes—some of them might, I mean."

"Ah, but to eliminate all such items would be both unrealistic and ultimately unfair to those committed to my care. They must learn to cope with such things as ammonia and automobiles."

"Computers," Tock Von said.

"I beg your pardon?"

"I've always had a thing for computers ever since I did my preliminary research into the workings of the human brain. I was hoping maybe Pomeroy could use me as an assistant. Taking care of that computer must be a big job for just one man."

Quest's eyes narrowed, widened. "We always seek to indulge our patient's desire whenever feasible and your suggestion is definitely feasible. You might even be able to contribute some imaginative ideas concerning possible programs to be designed for future dramas."

"Yep, I just might," Tock Von agreed, imagining his lion's jaws snapping toothily shut on an unwary jackal.

"Such a diversion is in the very finest tradition of occupational therapy. It will not only engage your mind with realistic problems but also channel your physical and psychic energies. Programmers are expensive these days."

Quest turned his head and called Pomeroy's name. Immediately, the man appeared in the doorway wearing his clean white coat and no smile. "Yes, Doctor?"

Quest edged closer to Pomeroy and began to explain that Novotck would be Pomeroy's unofficial but, he was confident, most competent and earnest assistant in the days to come.

Tock Von, as Quest's explanation unfolded, thought that Miss Dear was right. They were everywhere, the Pomeroys. They were the interdenominational genies that responded to officialdom's lamp rubbing by popping promptly out from behind refrigerators, dropping down on sky hooks from dirigibles, or bursting through barred or unbarred doors when the proper call came. In their white coats or green wigs, they were always ready, Tock Von told himself, and it was no wonder, none, that the Miss Dears of the world walked with trepidation and no little unease.

"—something original," Quest was saying. "Some sort of program that will allow our guests to sample conflictual situations. Pomeroy, use Novotck. Explore with him any ideas he might have for our Arena programing. Patient participation is to be desired, um."

"Thank you," Tock Von said to Quest. "I'm sorry if I ripped you off before. I guess I was—shook about what happened to Mueller."

"No harm done," Quest declared. "The human mind is a mountain range full of emotional peaks and valleys. Good luck to you!"

Pomeroy's eyes remained on Tock Von after Quest had

left the room. "Are you familiar with computer program ing, Novotck?"

"No. But I could learn. I've been thinking that maybe I ought to get my head into something really realistic and computers—well, they're where your world is at, right?"

"Our world? Oh, I see. Would you like to begin now? I suppose I shall first have to arrange matters so that your retinal pattern will open the Arena door."

"Fine. Let's do it."

They went and did it.

In the days that followed, Tock Von learned the difference between analog and digital computers. He discovered with Pomeroy's help that the on-off switching of the Arena's digital computer's logic circuits could be clocked at close to a billionth of a second. Said Pomeroy at one point, "One billionth of a second is to one second as one second is to thirty years." Tock Von marveled sufficiently to satisfy Pomeroy and the instructions went on. Transistors were touched, memory banks examined, semiconductors were allowed to conduct bits of information that would transform the Arena into a circus or a hell depending upon what mathematical descriptions were placed on the hundreds of punched cards Pomeroy fed to the hungry machine.

Depending upon those odd mathematical descriptions, the Arena filled with buildings, with a swamp, with suddenly activated plastic people, or even, in one remarkable demonstration, with Wordsworthian daffodils.

Pomeroy patiently explained to the patient in his therapeutic care the methods by which mathematics could be manipulated to create from available materials a cloud, a tree, a tent, a stone. All materials used in the Arena's scenes—the fiberboard, the polymers, the hundreds of other elements—were subject to the process control of the computer which, as Pomeroy explained its intricate operation, he fondled like a lover with a mechanical mistress who was both obedient and provocatively enterprising.

Throughout the Arena, according to Pomeroy, were sensors which fed back data to the computer's memory banks. They in turn checked the feedback of the program to be created with a basic set of instructions also stored in the memory banks and they then transmitted a return signal to the sensor network which resulted in the creation of, for example, Gideon, Ohio or Universal University.

"Amazing," Tock Von said, adding a veneer of ersatz awe to his voice to hide his growing excitement. "Out of sight!"

Pomeroy blushed and touched the cool surface of the machine. "Out of sight," he repeated reverently.

"Information then," he went on in a hushed tone, "is the fuel on which the computer runs. It is the machine's mind, so to speak. The programs designed by Doctor Quest are recorded on magnetic tape—here." He pointed. "Each item to be used—the buildings, the streets, whatever—are coded in specific mathematical symbols. Each symbol is then recorded on the tape in a complex series of minute magnetized dots. One has only to use the proper symbols in the proper sequence and one can create—anything!"

Tock Von let his lower jaw drop an inch, his eyebrows rise two.

Pomeroy nodded.

"A palace?"

"Anything!" Pomeroy's eyes glowed. His pale tongue flicked along his upper lip, leaving upon it a sheen of saliva. He explained to Tock Von how the mathematical symbols were created. He pointed proudly to the network of sensors throughout the Arena which carried the feedback and the feedforward.

When two more days had passed, Tock Von was convinced he was ready to make his move. Guile was not his natural way of dealing with matters or organisms in his natural milieu, but this was Earth, not Eleison, and he had long ago learned that humans hustled both themselves and each other. It was clearly the humanistic thing to do.

Pomeroy insisted upon overseeing Tock Von's first efforts at the creation of a program for the Arena. It was a simple affair—a commune modeled in large part on a kibbutz he had surveyed while masquerading as an Israeli Hebrew teacher during his very first terrestrial field trip.

Pomeroy placed Tock Von's program in the computer, and the dust that rose up from the floor choked them both. A devouring sun glared down from the simulated sky. Plastic Arabs in burnooses rode knob-kneed camels through the dust, pausing now and then to sprinkle phosphates in the kibbutz's irrigation canals.

"Your program offers only limited scope," Pomeroy chided, gagging on the dust that swirled through his sinuses. "A really successful program must provide its participants with far greater scope for their own improvisations and creativities. Deserts are rather limited in those respects. But it is interesting. Yes, it is an interesting first attempt."

"I suppose I need more practice," Tock Von admitted modestly. "I'll try again."

Carrying a chart containing the mathematical combinations for items presently available in the Arena scenarios and more than a mile of virginal magnetic tape, Tock Von took up position in an empty corner of the Arena. He had told Pomeroy that he had conceived a scenario to end all scenarios. Doctor Quest, he said, would find it most remarkable. Could he work on it alone? Would Pomeroy grant him the gift of freedom to create his new program and present it as a surprise to Doctor Quest in a private—? What word to use? "A private screening, Pom?"

Pomeroy, pleased with his pupil's enthusiastic progress, agreed to let Tock Von proceed in freedom and privacy. He insisted upon only one qualification. He himself must first run the program through to see that it was "suitable" before it could be shown to Doctor Quest.

"That's cool," was Tock Von's cooperative response after which he went to work, thinking of Medea and Oedipus. Earth's Sophocles and Euripides had known that tragedy began as a seed that a man carried within him and which awaited the day when the season would be right, and the sun and rains kind, before it blossomed, causing the murder of children and the gouging out of royal eyes.

Quest, thought Tock Von, I shall bring rain to your garden and send a sun to smile upon it, so that the seed you harbor may burst forth into full and evil bloom here in the fabulous Lost City of the Insane.

The work went slowly but well. Like a painter with two clear eyes on the world, Tock Von looked about the Arena, measuring and gauging, and then bent to the magnetic tape and punched in the mathematics, symbol by shrewd symbol, until the program he had conceived days ago took shape on the bland face of the tape lying so innocently beneath his wily hands.

Monica found him winding the tape the next day in a corner of the Arena. She came up to him and spoke his name softly. He waited for her to go on, watching her face, noting the way her eyelashes flickered. When she did not or could not speak, he said, "I've missed you."

The words seemed to lighten whatever burden Monica was bearing. Her eyes brightened and the tenseness of her stance eased.

"It's good to see you," she said. "I looked for you and when I couldn't find you, I asked Doctor Quest about you. He told me you were here. I was surprised when he said you were working for him."

"Surprised? Why?"

"Because—When we were—together the other day, you said you didn't think I should cooperate with Doctor Quest. You said you thought it would be wrong. I didn't really understand everything you said then."

"But now? Now, Monica?"

"I wake up in the night. I see Mr. Mueller—his body—lying—" She looked into the huge emptiness of the Arena and back at the door which Tock Von had left open in order to avoid arousing Pomeroy's suspicions.

Tock Von put his hands on her upper arms. "On Eleison, when one of us dies, we make music. We make joyful music to celebrate the returning of the one who has left us to his essence. We sing."

"Here on Earth, we weep," Monica said.

"I know. Humans let themselves know more of pain

than of joy. They have not learned to celebrate the changes their lives take. They are more skilled at mourning than at celebration. But children grow up."

"Some of us don't. Some of us hide from the years and the changes they bring."

"Hiding works for awhile. But the hiders are usually found and then the game enters a new phase."

"You're going back, aren't you? You said you were."

"To Eleison? Yes, I'm going home."

"Alone."

Tock Von hesitated. What if—? But he knew it was impossible. The trip through the return warp would be fatal to a human being. "Alone," he said.

Monica turned away from him to stare without seeing into the Arena's emptiness. "When I was a child, I never lived in the present. I was always waiting for—oh, for Saturday to come, because on Saturday I had been promised a new bicycle. So Tuesday and all the other days didn't matter at all while I waited for Saturday to come. It came. So did the new bicycle and I was happy. But then it was Sunday all of a sudden and the bicycle wasn't quite so new anymore. I heard that the circus was coming to our town. I watched the men put up the posters all over town and I got my sister—she was three years older than I was—to read the date to me—you know, the date the circus would arrive. I went home and made a red circle around the day on our kitchen calendar. I waited and waited, and at last the circus came. For a time, the lions and tigers, the bareback riders, and all the handsome aerialists filled my world. But next day, they were gone.

"One day I took the calendar down from the kitchen wall and I counted all the days that I had circled in red. There were five of them from January to May. Then I counted all the ordinary days and I realized that I had been cheating myself. My mother made me stay in my room alone that night while the family ate dinner without me. She couldn't understand why I had torn the calendar to shreds."

"Didn't you explain to her what you had discovered?"

"I didn't know how to explain. I was ashamed. How could I tell anyone—how could I dare tell anyone that I had really lived only five days in four months?"

As Monica moved toward him, as her body came to rest gently against his own, Tock Von said, "After the bicycle and the circus there came that other day. The day with the brightest red circle of all around it. The day he came."

"I hadn't even known I'd been waiting for him," Monica whispered.

"Monica, what was his name?"

He knew he had made a mistake as soon as he completed the question because her body stiffened against his. She stepped back. She refused to look at him.

"I'm sorry," he said, knowing clearly now how it felt to be human.

"I wish his name had been Tock Von."

"It wasn't." He had to say it even though he knew that by saying it he was sacrificing his own feelings on an already bloodied altar.

"Will you ever come back?" Monica asked as she folded her arms.

Tock Von noticed the white imprints on her flesh where her fingers rested so tightly. "Yes."

She looked up at him. "Then I'll see you again."

He couldn't lie, not totally. So he said, "Perhaps."

"Tock Von, I want to get out of here. I'm afraid to stay here now. Mr. Mueller—Miss Dear's broken arm— I'm really afraid of this place—and of Doctor Quest too."

"You should be."

"But it makes no sense, my fear. Doctor Quest is so sincere. He just wants to help us adjust to reality, to learn to deal with it. Why should I suddenly feel so afraid of him?"

"You're right," Tock Von said. "Doctor Quest is sincere. But beware of a man dedicated to reality and not to the possibility of altering that reality. Your fear is a signal that warns you of the beast walking in the night. Listen to your fear and take precautions."

"But what can I do? There's no way out of here."

"Yes, there is a way."

"What way?"

Giving her his spookiest-eyed glance, Tock Von said, "If you can't fight Quest, join him."

"I don't understand."

"You will. Now listen to me."

Monica listened. At times she protested that his plan would not, could not possibly work. He ignored her protests and explained in detail a second time exactly what he had in mind. He showed her the tape he had prepared and described the program he had created.

"I promised Pomeroy," he said, "that I'd let him check it out before it was actually used in the Arena. But I'm not going to show it to him. I'm going to feed it to that monster over there, and with a little help from my friends, we'll beat Quest at his own reality game."

"It's absurd," Monica said with a mixture of hope and despair.

"It is indeed," Tock Von readily agreed. "But it just might work. Will you help me?"

Monica took his face between her hands and kissed him on the lips. He pulled her close to him and the chasteness of their kiss rapidly gave way to a fiery passion that Tock Von knew must soon surrender to an inevitable Eleisonite goodby. As they remained momentarily bound together, he knew that the successful escape he sought would bring with it a singular failure. In the darkness behind his closed eyelids, he saw a sad someone and he could not at first believe it was himself. The someone was sobbing.

TWELVE

Doctor Is Out.

On the morning of the following day, with Chief One Wild Wolf standing watch outside the summerhouse, Tock Von went over the final plans for his assault on Excelsior with his co-conspirators.

"Now, Miss Dear," he said, "you will—"

"Hush!" cried Miss Dear, putting a slim finger to her slimmer lips as cigarette smoke suddenly swirled into the room.

Tock Von went to the door and looked out. He turned back to the others, winked, and began to wave his hands back and forth in the air, dissolving the smoke signals the Chief had blown their way to warn of the approach of an enemy.

"Row, row, row your boat," began Miss Dear shrilly.

"Gently down the stream," sang Papa Summerhall, winding one of his watches in time with the tune.

"Merrily, merrily, merrily, merrily," added Monica in a lilting voice, her eyes on the door.

"Life is but a dream," concluded Tock Von.

"It's okay now," the Chief muttered as he popped his

head through the door a minute later. "It was only Pomeroy. He's gone."

Papa Summerhall nodded. "I knew it was about time for Pomeroy to make a move."

Miss Dear snapped her teeth shut on a final "merrily" and told Tock Von to get on with it.

"We haven't got all day," Papa Summerhall said somewhat testily.

Tock Von, a shrewd Shylock rich with schemes, said, "I've explained to you about the program I designed for Pomeroy's computer. I've indicated what will result when it is activated. Each of you knows what to do when—"

"Timing is important," interrupted Papa Summerhall. "We must have split-second accuracy."

"You're right," Tock Von agreed. "We should all have watches."

Papa Summerhall sprang to his feet and began handing out watches. Miss Dear received a gold one in a snap-shut case. Monica's was set in silver. He went to the door of the summerhouse and hissed, *"Psstt!"*

When the Chief leaped to his side, he handed him a miniature alarm clock. "Let's synchronize," he said and, following Tock Von's approving nod, declared, "It is now eleven minutes and thirty one seconds past ten o'clock on the morning of Tuesday, the eighteenth day of the seventh month in the year nineteen hundred and—"

"Got it!" Tock Von said, setting the watch Papa Summerhall had given him, the one with the octopus painted on its face whose eight tentacles pointed to four sets of different times. "Okay, we're all synchronized now thanks to Papa Summerhall. At exactly nine minutes past two this afternoon, we'll execute our plan. Each of you has his or her job to perform. Now let's go over it one more time. Miss Dear?"

Miss Dear rapidly repeated her instructions in the binary code she shared with Tock Von, and he in turn translated her words for the benefit of the others.

Monica expressed some doubts about being able to properly execute her part of the plan, but Papa Summerhall quickly assured her that time was on her side and so she was not to worry.

"Chief!" Tock Von called. "You know what you're supposed to do?"

The Chief said he knew.

"Right on!" Tock Von exulted, his mind blown with eerie plans.

"Excelsior's time has come!" intoned Papa Summerhall in a deep voice of doom.

"Ssshhh!" Miss Dear commanded, looking about her. "There's no telling where they might be hiding, and if they hear us— Oh, I hate to think of what might happen." She lifted the calico skirt on the wicker couch and peeped nervously underneath it.

"Tock Von," Monica ventured, "do you really think it will work?"

"Our plan? Of course. It has an Eleisonite simplicity combined with a terrestrial duplicity that makes it a sure thing. Okay, that's it for now. Remember—at nine minutes after two this afternoon, everyone must be at his station. Papa Summerhall and Miss Dear will form Squad One. Monica, Squad Two." He noted the way Monica's face darkened as she caught the implications of being the lone member of a Squad that was designated number two, the latter number one Tock Von suspected would soon again become significant in her life. "Chief One Wild Wolf and I will form Squad Three."

"To the barricades!" piped Miss Dear, both fists high in the air. "Long live LUST!"

After the others had left the summerhouse, Monica turned to Tock Von and said, "You really aren't human, are you?"

"No, I'm not."

"It's ironic," she mused. "You're the most human—maybe the word is humane—being I've ever met. You give love; you don't use it."

"Some humans, I've learned, are the same way."

"The return warp you mentioned—is there really such a thing?"

He laughed. "Yes, there really is such a thing despite

what the Quests of your world might say. Come on, Monica! Don't look so solemn! You look more like an owl than a beautiful young girl. Smile at me. Laugh out loud with me. You don't want to remember only frowns when I—" He stopped.

"When you go."

He forced his smile to remain on his face.

At last Monica let herself laugh. The sound swept through the summerhouse, and if there was a hint of a remembered winter within it, it nevertheless made Tock Von think of clover and soft spring rains.

"It's much better," he assured her, "to remember laughter than tears."

They left together a moment later, after bringing their bodies together briefly, after linking their lips in a silent language they had learned together, a language that was as ancient as Earth itself.

"I'll be outside Quest's door to help you bring him down," Tock Von told Monica just before they separated. "If anything goes wrong, I'll be right there. So don't worry."

He watched her walk across the lawn. He saw her hesitate momentarily and then walk briskly on without looking back. He wanted to call her name to cause her to turn toward him so that he might see one more time that lovely face that had brought a sun to illuminate his midnights but he refrained.

He glanced at the watch Papa Summerhall had given him. In a little more than one hour . . .

Excelsior was quiet. Only a lonely wind moved about the grounds, slipping through the trees as if in search of something. Mrs. Daley was nowhere in sight. Neither was Pomeroy. Drapes were drawn across the broad expanse of Quest's office windows on the ground floor of the main building. No bird sang anywhere.

Tock Von sat down beneath a beech tree. Home, he thought. Eleison, where love was not bought or sold, where myths were honored and every Eleisonite was his own magician who conjured peace which he dispensed with humility. Eleison. Earth. He recalled the sense of superiority he had felt when he had taken his first trip to Earth. Barbarism, he had thought from the high throne of his mind as he surveyed the cities and the streets, the bedrooms and the banks, the pulpits. He had sneered, had mocked. The put-on and the bring-down had been his weapons. His research had progressed satisfactorily. He had stayed uncommitted. People generally either amused or horrified him. He turned them on and tuned them out as it suited his current purposes. Occasionally other members of the Expeditionary Force chastised him for his scorn, urging compassion on him. Look how humans suffer, one had told him. Centuries, that one had told him, would have to pass before humans would find the strength to give and take love that would put an end to pain. He had brushed the concept of compassion aside. He was a researcher, he had argued. Only that. The members of the Expedition, he recalled, had smiled at his response. But he had ignored the smiles. He had ahead of him, after all, all the years. . . .

All the years.

What was happening to him? He was thinking like a human being. Like a foreigner who learns the odd vowels and tricky consonants of an unfamiliar language, he was using concepts like *years* that were irrelevant on Eleison. Was this then one result of contact with another life form? Was it an infection? Was it a drug? How had it come about? Remembering the cocktail party he had been researching—Sister Sappho and her twisted desire for the waitress from New Rochelle, recalling the brittle blonde about to rip off the drunken advertising executive's wallet—he also remembered Monica. And something else. He remembered the something that was often an adjunct to the sale of often shoddy merchandise. He had felt it surge within the phallus that adorned his strange body. No, it was not love he had felt in the intricate workings of his glands. What he had felt was desire, the handmaiden of love, the gypsied sorceress who spoke a language of lust. But still— With Monica, he had felt something else. It was undoubtedly desire but, yes, something more, something quite beyond that red peak of glandular passion. Love? But he was letting her go. After guiding her through the mists in which the name she feared was hidden, he was letting her go despite the fact that he could stay awhile longer and let her love him. But it would be wrong, he reasoned. He would be little more than a competent thief stealing from Monica a dimension which, once she had acknowledged it, would let her move on to higher mountains where the view was not only dazzling but liberating.

As he thought of liberation, he thought of the return warp and of going home, a liberation from all things human, a return to himself. But— How long had it been since the party he and all the others had been researching? Weeks. A sudden chill seized him and shook him in its icy teeth. What was the warning the Commander had given him as he fought to free himself from her grip in order to move out into Earth and see more than the restricted schedule the Expedition permitted? He didn't want to think about it. An urgency bubbled up in him. He rose from the bench and began to walk quickly toward the main building where Quest was hidden behind the drawn damask drapes of his office.

He had almost reached the building when Papa Summerhall's mysterious superclock hidden in the old man's room within the structure began to boom in a voice thick with time and telling of destiny.

Two o'clock.

Nine more minutes. Monica, he thought. In nine minutes you will come to Quest and the world of Excelsior will turn and turn and nothing will ever again be the same for any of us.

The voice of Papa Summerhall's clock whined its way into silence as Tock Von took up his planned position in the small alcove diagonally across from Quest's office door.

A long nine minutes; an eternity of time.

But an eternity with an end. Monica came down the corridor, her eyes on Quest's door. Tock Von stepped out of the alcove. She saw him and nodded. She began to sob. Tock Von, watching her, found her performance perfectly convincing. He would certainly comfort such a maiden after her encounter with a dragon. So, he was sure, would Quest, the dragon, try to comfort his victim, a mild variation on a mythic theme.

She entered the office, leaving the door slightly ajar. Tock Von moved close to it. Two thirteen. Listening . . .

". . . can't bear it anymore, Doctor. I'll never . . ."

"My dear Monica, whatever is the matter? You were doing so well too. Tears, my dear? What has? . . ."

The next words were muffled. Had she so quickly flung herself against Quest?

"Monica, Monica. . . ."

"I really need something to help me relax. I don't sleep. I have such terrible dreams. Men with no names demand that I . . ."

"I don't like to use drugs, as you know. They disorient one. Reality is softened, not experienced. But you seem so . . ."

"Please . . ."

The sound of water running.

"Here, my dear. Take one of these. The others are for the days to come."

"Thank you, Doctor."

Beat.

"But we should drink a toast, Doctor. To us. Please?"

Tock Von saw Quest move to fill the inch of space between the door and the jamb, vanish, and then return, a glass of water in his hands.

"Oh, Doctor!"

A touching of glass to glass . . .

Two eighteen.

As two twenty-seven arrived, Monica appeared and said, "He's—resting comfortably. I put the tranquilizing powders in his water. Four of them. I saved them as you told me to. He's sound asleep."

Tock Von slipped into the office to stare down at the mound of man lying on the leather sofa, his medical hands at rest, his green glasses tilting at an odd angle on his nose. He removed Quest's glasses and set them carefully on the desk.

"Shall we use this?" Monica asked, holding up a printed sign.

Doctor Is Out.

Tock Von laughed and took the sign from her. After they had slipped out of the office, he slipped the sign into the metal slot on the door.

Doctor Is Out.

"Right on," he said, saluting the sign and then he and Monica ran down the hall.

They found Chief One Wild Wolf in the cafeteria, loudly demanding that he be fed and never mind the goddam fact that it was not officially mealtime. Pomeroy, quite obviously and sadistically enjoying the Chief's feigned distress, continued calmly counting his spoons.

"Rhubarb!" roared the Chief. "Sirloin steak. Enroll me in a poverty program! I'm starving!"

"Twenty-seven," said Pomeroy to a spoon. "Lunch is always served at twelve sharp. Twenty-eight, twenty-nine . . ."

"Pig's feet!" the Chief shouted when he spotted Tock Von. The agreed upon code word rang through the empty cafeteria to join its lyrics to the score of the thirty some spoons clinking in Pomeroy's pack rat paws.

"Stay away from me!" Pomeroy moaned as Tock Von moved swiftly toward him. "Doctor Quest does not condone violence as a way of dealing with personal problems. Stay away and make an adjustment!"

The Chief brought an empty casserole down on Pomeroy's shoulders. The blow sent both spoons and Pomeroy crashing to the floor. Tock Von grabbed the velveteen ropes that made a neat path beside the steam tables. With the Chief's expert help, he tied the ropes around Pomeroy's wrists and ankles until the man lay gasping on the shore of his no longer safe beach.

"Mrs. Daley!" Pomeroy bellowed from his hard bed of fallen spoons. "Doctor Quest!"

"Doctor Quest is out," Tock Von yelled back as Miss

Dear tore through the cafeteria in flight from an invisible pursuer.

"Mrs. Daley!" screamed Miss Dear. "They're after me! Oh, Mrs. Daley, you must help me! We women must—"

She leaped over the fallen Pomeroy and ran on toward Papa Summerhall who had popped in at the door. "Two twenty-eight!" he yelped at the top of his voice. "Mrs. Daley, where the hell are you, you old amazon?"

He took Miss Dear's uninjured arm and they ran from the cafeteria as Pomeroy began to threaten Tock Von, Monica and the Chief with isolation rooms and other assorted disasters.

"Chief," said Tock Von, pointing to the refrigerator behind the cafeteria counter.

The Chief vaulted the counter, opened the refrigerator, and returned with a huge bowl of rice pudding which he spooned into Pomeroy's mouth to silence him. Then, with Monica leading the way, Tock Von and the Chief carried the spitting and spluttering Pomeroy out of the cafeteria, across the hall and into the Arena after Tock Von had blinked its door open.

"Next," said Tock Von, "Quest."

The Chief ran to Quest's office and tossed the sleeping sackful of flesh over one broad shoulder and came loping back into the Arena where he deposited the doctor on the floor beside Pomeroy.

"It's about time," Tock Von began, "for—"

"There they are!" Miss Dear screeched, pointing into the Arena.

Papa Summerhall sidled up to Tock Von. "We're not late, are we?"

Tock Von shook his head as Mrs. Daley, who was standing beside Miss Dear, let out a startled and wordless exclamation as she stared at her colleagues on the floor.

"I never trusted charity cases!" she declared. "Mr. Novotck, what is the—?"

Papa Summerhall swung open the storage room door near the Arena's entrance. Miss Dear apologized to Mrs. Daley for what she was about to do to a potential member of LUST, and then she gave the woman a one-handed shove that sent her reeling into the closet. Papa Summerhall slammed the door behind her and locked it.

"Phase Two," Tock Von announced, grinning. He went to the computer, opened a panel in its base and slid out the reel that held the program he had so carefully and conscientiously designed. "Everybody step back please."

When he had inserted the reel and closed the glass door shielding the technological mysteries from dust and other intruders, he reached in his pocket and then began to pass out balls of bubble gum. Soon, everyone was chewing as the Arena convulsed almost as if in protest and the program unwound itself to create . . .

"Look!" Monica cried. "It's working!"

"A second Arena," the Chief marveled. "One wasn't bad enough."

"Watch!" Tock Von ordered them.

Within minutes, the vast expanse of the original Arena was filled with a second one which fit easily and neatly within its walls. Within the programmed Arena, Quest lay peacefully, a sleeper lost in his drugged dream. Pomeroy continued to spit grains of white rice in a wet snow all about him as he tried to make his tongue and teeth work together in a hopelessly rice-ridden speech.

Tock Von gave his instructions and everyone inserted their bubble gum into the switches and dials of the computer. "That should keep it running automatically for a while," he declared when their task was completed. "It will keep running indefinitely now. Okay. Everybody outside. Phase Three is about to begin."

After closing the Arena door, they gathered in front of the one-way glass that let them see into the Arena within the Arena.

"Doctor Quest—" Monica began, pointing.

"He's waking up," the Chief observed.

As they all watched, a dismayed Quest struggled to his feet and then dropped down on his portly knees beside Pomeroy. Tock Von began to whistle softly.

Miss Dear, recognizing the tune, crooned, "Merrily, merrily, merrily—"

Quest untied Pomeroy and helped him swallow the last of the rice. They rose together and looked about the Arena.

Tock Von and the others listened to the faint echoes of the voices coming through the grill in the wall next to the window.

"We've got to find them!" from Quest.

"Felons all," Pomeroy muttered furiously. "Fugitives everyone!"

Tock Von placed an arm around Monica's shoulder, drawing her closer to him.

Quest started into the Arena but the sudden pounding on the closet door caused him to halt and turn top-like to the source of the sound. When he and Pomeroy had released an indignant Mrs. Daley, they made their plans.

They would hunt down the felon-fugitives. It was obviously the only and the ethical thing to do.

They moved deeper into the Arena.

Tock Von squeezed Monica's hand as the three pilgrims unwittingly moved into another Arena.

"That one—that Arena within the Arena within the Arena—it has its own computer," Tock Von declared to the delight of the others watching. "And, as I told you, that computer contains a duplicate of the original program I created so it will create still another Arena. And that one will create still another! The only limitation to the plot is the space within the original Arena and it's got lots!"

"Oh!" from a delighted Monica. "It really did work. Look at them. They're getting farther and farther away."

"From reality," said Tock Von a bit smugly. "Let's split."

"Where to?" Monica asked.

"The helicopter, of course," he replied. "Up, up and away from the fabulous Lost City of the Insane."

With a war-whooping Chief One Wild Wolf in the lead, they ran from the building toward the mauve hangar where the red helicopter sat waiting. It took Tock Von and Papa Summerhall some time to decipher the control panel that was the mind of the remote controlled machine.

But finally, with the help of the tools in Papa Summerhall's watch repair kit, they managed to jam the control panel on ON.

Once inside the plane, they fastened their seat belts and held their collective breaths. A shuddering. A mechanical sigh. The helicopter lumbered out of the hangar and then up into the idyllic air. Its blades sliced through the air, its motor droned deafeningly.

The section at the top of the dome lifted; they flew through it; it closed behind them. A moment later, the helicopter landed on its oily pad not far from the curved skin of the dome. They disembarked and Monica, looking around her at trees and hearing the songs of real birds, asked, "What now?"

Miss Dear, thinking the question had been addressed to her, replied, "Did I ever tell you? LUST sponsors and maintains a perfectly lovely home for wayward girls. I shall go there at once. I shall be quite comfortable—and safe—there."

"Tock Von," said the Chief, "there's a group of red militants on the Iroquois reservation here in New York State. I'll bet they'd be glad to have the benefit of my experience in dealing with the wily white man's world. Come with me, man! We could use a guy with your brains and balls!"

The Chief promptly apologized for his last word, and Miss Dear indignantly withdrew her hands from her ears. Monica suppressed a smile. Papa Summerhall, who had been holding a watch to his ear, said, "I've found the secret. It was so simple! I should have thought of it time and time again."

"The secret?" Tock Von prompted.

"Look!" Papa Summerhall proudly held out the watch to which he had been listening.

Tock Von leaned forward. The watch, he noted, contained the essential twelve numerals but with a difference. They had been rearranged so that they ran counterclockwise. As did the watch's tiny hands.

"Backward," Papa Summerhall explained. "Turn time around. Recapture the past. Why, already I feel ten years younger. I remember a girl I knew once." He looked fondly at his watch. "Seems like I knew her only yesterday. Beautiful little thing. All brown eyes and dimples. In a short time—by *this* watch—I should be able to see her again for sure."

Tock Von smiled.

"So what do you say, my man?" the Chief asked him. "Join our Red Liberation Movement."

"I've—I can't. I've got to—go home." Tock Von offered his hand to the Chief who took it, held it a moment, and then gave a wave and another war whoop, and vanished among the trees.

"Miss Dear," Tock Von said. "I wish you and LUST all sorts of earthly success."

Miss Dear fiercely wiped the wetness from her eyes and kissed him on the cheek with an equal fierceness. "If I were younger," she told him in a whisper, "why, I might even reconsider my position vis-a-vis male chauvinism but as it is—"

Tock Von kissed her old cheek and she turned away from him and strode resolutely down the road, looking back now and then, waving happily, marching on to the tune of some inner martial music. Tock Von blinked; she disappeared behind a tree. He thought he saw her flying one-winged through the trees but he couldn't be sure.

"I have so much to do," Papa Summerhall announced solemnly. "Now that my watch runs more satisfactorily—well, I really must be going. Dammit, there is simply never enough time to be with the people one has learned to love."

Tock Von felt himself smothered in the old man's sudden embrace. "I want to return the watch you gave me, Papa Summerhall," he said, holding out the octopus-faced mechanism he had taken from his pocket.

"Keep it. I've no further use for that one. Not now. Not since I've found out how watches really ought to run. I might even patent my invention. I could make a million. Mueller would be proud of me. Think of all the people who have lost other people in all the years. The market for such a watch would be unlimited!"

He walked briskly down the road toward the highway.

When he had disappeared around the bend in the road, Tock Von said, "Are you ready to go, Monica?"

"I think so."

As they walked beneath green trees that split the sun into slivers of light, Tock Von was silent. He knew he was waiting for something, but he was not quite sure what that something was.

"Do you have a knife?" Monica asked him.

"Nope. A nailfile though. Will that do?"

She took it from him and went up to an old tree. It took her some time to complete her task. When she did, Tock Von joined her at the tree and examined her handiwork.

"I loved him," Monica said. "But despite what Papa Summerhall's watch says, I can't go back to him."

"You loved him," Tock Von said, knowing now what he had been waiting for. "His name was Steve."

"I love you."

"You loved Steve. You love me. Now that you have let yourself know the truth, you will love again."

"I think I had better go on by myself," Monica said.

"I think you're right."

"Have a good trip home."

"It has been a very good trip here," Tock Von told her. "I wouldn't have missed it for your world."

Alone.

Papa Summerhall was gone in search of yesterday. Miss Dear was once again in hiding from all those who would take her moving picture because she believed in what they did not. Chief One Wild Wolf had embarked once again on his own particular warpath as he sought to prove the proposition that thieves talked in elegant English and wore expensive clothes. Monica was already at home in a hopeful tomorrow.

Alone, Tock Von walked down the road to the highway. He did not look back at Excelsior in which he had not ever and did not now really believe.

After reaching the highway, it took him ten minutes to get a reaction to his raised thumb. His first chauffeur was a man with a tic in his forever twisting cheek and a confirmed belief in astrology who told Tock Von that anyone born in a place called Eleison was definitely fated for fame. The second car that picked him up contained a woman with stiff hair who kept talking about how tired she was and how she needed to stop at a motel. When she did, Tock Von declined her invitation and once again raised his thumb.

Thus, by way of astrology and along a detour marked by muted nymphomania, he reached his destination.

Thumbs, he knew, although an interesting anthropoid appendage, were useless as stimulants to transportation in the spired and phallic field of buildings that was New York City. He walked. He walked past derelicts asleep in doorways and other derelicts wide awake and on their feet, running for taxis and their lives.

When he finally reached the apartment that had contained the cocktail party the Eleisonite Expeditionary Force had been researching—how many ages ago?—he knocked on its door.

A key turning in a lock. A bolt sliding back. The door opening an inch, held together by a slim hand and a chain lock.

"Excuse me," he said, "but I—"

One blue eye peering out. A piece of cheek and a bit of a rather pert nose. Perfume, provocative. Blond hair, straight down an unseen back.

"My name is—" Never mind. Not now.

"I'm all alone," she said through the full lips beneath the appraising blue eye. "My roommate—she's out so—"

"I just want to use your phone. This is not a hustle. Do I look like a hustler?"

"I'm all alone."

"Just your phone, okay?"

"Okay, I guess." The chain slid back. The door opened to reveal five and a half feet of female who looked like she could take very good care of herself. Tock Von decided that if such as she were the ilk of ancient Christians thrown to Roman lions, the Christians would have converted the beasts within minutes.

While she made Turkish coffee, he pretended to use the telephone, all the while easing toward the return warp, invisible in its space time slot next to the bedroom door. One foot, then the other. Nothing. Moving all the way in with determination. Nothing.

"Are you nervous," she asked, miniature coffee cups held in both hands, "or is that some new kind of dance step you're doing?"

He didn't answer. Couldn't. Where the hell was the return warp? He tried again. Still nothing. Not panic but a sense of mild frustration swept over him. What had the Commander said? In time, the return warp would decoalesce. Was that cool? Maybe. He looked down at his only pair of pants courtesy of Questian enterprises, at his square white shirt and funky shoes. He sighed.

She said, "I do whatever I like."

"Everybody has to feed their own head," he responded.

"You'll dig what I do."

Later, the coffee cold in the untouched cups, while she and Tock Von, their heads and bodies together, did it and dug it, he heard her say in the darkness of her bedroom, "My name is Lois."

Almost automatically, with a typical Eleisonite honesty, he responded somewhat sleepily, "Hi, Lois. My name's—"

No, she wouldn't believe it and he didn't want to argue. So he reached out for her again, and she eagerly let herself be found.

Outside in the New York night, Earth turned unnoticeably. Inside the bedroom, the worlds of Tock Von and Lois turned in response to an equally undeniable force in which was encapsuled, for Tock Von, a warm memory of Monica.

Afterward, Lois said to him, "Hey, man. Don't go."

"I can't go," he said. "I mean I won't go."

"Groovy," she said.

"Come here," he said, wondering what another earthly tomorrow would bring down on him.

She came.